If One of Us Should Die, I'll Move to Paris

Brandon French

Tolsun Books

Tolleson, Arizona and Las Vegas, Nevada

If One of Us Should Die, I'll Move to Paris

ISBN 978-1-948800-17-4

Published by Tolsun Books, LLC
Tolleson, Arizona and Las Vegas, Nevada

www.tolsunbooks.com

"What's the secret of comed—?"

"Timing."

CONTENTS

Acknowledgments

Thank you to the editors of the journals and anthologies who previously published the following stories:

"You Don't Give Dogs Champagne," *Riverlit*

"The Big Book of Kitty Porn," *The Ottowa Object*

"Her Hair," *Sequestrum*

"The Ice Cream Cone," *Riverlit*

"Tall," *Constellations* and *Musewrite*

"Exhibition Eater," *Flights* and *The Way to My Heart*

"He Had a Hat," *Slippery Elm*

"Elavil," *The Subterranean Review*

"A Lion Only Springs Once," *Calliope*

"Death Car Girl," *ThriceFiction*

"Bathing Beauty," *The Nassau Review*

"Mothership Down," *Hart House Review* and *Precipice*

"Falling Off the Turnip Truck," *Calliope*

"Locked in the Bathroom at The Actors Studio," *Blue Lyra*

"Mauschwitz," *Bete Noir*

This book is dedicated to Dr. Albert Mason, who said, "You can write your way out of this," and Lou Mathews, who taught me how to do that.

You Don't Give Dogs Champagne

My niece Trudy calls me and says, I'm getting married, and I say, To who? and she says, What do you mean, to who? To Sam! and I say, The one who slept with his sister for eight years? and she says, That's over now.

My sister Leslie, Trudy's mother, comes to my office building in Santa Monica to get money for a mother-of-the-bride dress. I won't let her come up to my office, I'm a legal secretary for one of the partners at a big law firm that represents all kinds of famous people like Jay Leno and Warren Beatty and I don't want them to know anything about my family. Sure enough Leslie shows up in a dirty white tee shirt, size XXXL, that says Pig Farmers Never Starve, and of course no bra, which means her boobs are playing rugby with each other whenever she moves, and she's holding a Bucket O' Soda, because a Big Gulp isn't big enough. And she's with her boyfriend Andrew–her husband Dave's away in prison for armed robbery. Andrew, a good old boy from Autaugaville, Alabama, with a face like a vanilla Moon Pie, weighs 300 pounds and is not wearing a shirt.

It's too hot for a shirt, Dolly, he whines, flexing his chest muscles to make his breast tattoos shimmy.

Bubbie can't find her teeth, Leslie says, taking two twenties and a ten from me. Our grandmother Bubbie lives with Leslie now that my mother's dating again.

Well, I don't have them, I say.

The wedding is next Saturday afternoon at the back of a travel agency in a mini-mall in Panorama City, screened off from the posters of Turkey and Argentina by a portable mural depicting The Last Supper, with apostles that look like the Mexican Mafia and a supper of enchiladas and frijoles.

Leslie has managed to score a mother-of-the-bride dress that looks like its last job was transporting Idaho potatoes; I figure most of the fifty I gave her went to Andrew's oxycontin habit. The groom's mother, an amateur porn actress named Cowgirl Kim, is wearing a two-piece powder blue cheerleader's outfit with white faux leather fringe. Her boyfriend, whose professional name is The Tongue, is surprisingly underdressed in a tweed sport coat and trousers. Only his leopard print loafers tip you off that he's in show biz.

As you might expect, the bride looks like Backwoods Barbie, clutching her little poodle Spanx and an enormous bouquet of blue plastic hydrangeas. I have brought the wedding gift that she and Sam requested, a Fry Daddy large enough for turkeys.

Do dju Trooby promet to lub Sam in sickens and helf? the priest, or proprietor, or the Captain of the Enterprise asks.

Woof, says Spanx.

Leslie leans over and whispers in my ear, They spelled Trudy's name wrong on the cake, Dolly.

I thought they didn't put names on wedding cakes, I say.

She raises her savagely plucked eyebrows at me and shrugs.

I look around at the guests, all of whom are standing because there are no chairs. Bubbie (who thank God found her teeth), my sister, my mother, my niece and the kids, three of whom are Leslie's, the flotsam of a half-dozen botched relationships, married and otherwise, and I wonder, how did I get into this ragtag family? And, more importantly, how do I get out?

My mother and Bubbie are crying now and saying what a beautiful ceremony. I am trying not to laugh. My mother, who recently had her eyes lifted, tries to give me a dirty look but it's too painful. I pull myself together and concentrate on Doubting Thomas in the mural pouring hot sauce on a burrito.

After the ceremony Leslie says, I used to be skinnier than you are when we were kids. She is looking at me in my size 4 silk wrap dress with big brown mournful eyes.

Hey, Les, I say, feeling bad for her because she's my big sister and I love her but the truth is she'd probably be pregnant by Alabama Andrew if my mother hadn't convinced her to have her tubes tied after the fourth kid.

You look great, I lie, and she knows it's a lie but she smiles anyway.

Staring at all the Mexican food imagery has made me hungry for some frijoles, but the reception is next door at the Korean barbecue. Korean? I say to my mother like did you have to? She says, When you're rich we'll go to The Olive Garden, which she considers the pinnacle of gourmet. I remind her as we're waiting in line to order that I'm a vegetarian and probably can't have the food.

Oh yes you can, she says, all superior like she knows something I don't know. The Koreans don't use real meat, she says.

Oh, really, ma? What kind of meat do they use? I ask, wondering what lie she's going to tell to get me to eat.

And you know what she says, like *yum*, get ready to be hungry?

Cats.

The Big Book of Kitty Porn

Adele owed $13,261 in overdue property taxes to L.A. County, which she, at the age of 68 and living on a monthly Social Security check and a small pension, had absolutely no way of paying. That's why she did it, I explained to our shocked friends at the Westwood United Methodist Church. She didn't want to lose her house.

The book was just a lot of pictures of her cats that she took with her iphone camera in sexy positions, which they get into naturally when they're cleaning themselves or sleeping because cats are shameless, and also very flexible. She said the idea came to her in a dream.

The picture that people were making the most fuss about was Elagabalus, the big Maine Coon cat, sitting on Wonker's face, but all they were doing was wrestling with one another, it just *looked* kind of naughty. And I suppose people were also having problems with Ms. Sadie cleaning Marx's belly with her tongue, but you'd have to have a pretty filthy mind to make something sexual about that, especially since both cats were neutered.

Adele self-published the book and in less than two weeks it was Amazon's #7 top-selling ebook. But no matter how I explained it, our church friends were still troubled, especially after Janice Goodrich googled the book on her Mac and got sent to a bunch of actual pornography sites, one of which involved donkeys.

Adele is my best friend but she didn't breathe a word to me about the book until after it came out, I guess because she was afraid I'd try to talk her out of it, and I surely would have. Our minister, Harold Potter, said he received 14 phone calls about it in one evening. He told everyone to pray for Adele and to refrain from making harsh judgments about another parishioner, which I think was very Christian of him.

But I really didn't know what I was going to say yesterday when I went over to Adele's house. I had wanted to wait until I had charitable thoughts, but she was so busy talking to agents and publishers who wanted to re-launch the book commercially that she didn't have any time for me until yesterday anyway.

When I let myself in, she was on her hands and knees on the living room floor. I thought for a minute that she had fallen down or had a stroke, but she said, "Hang on, Virginia, I'm finishing this article on the best investment bets for seniors."

"Why are you reading it on the floor?"

"Jefferson pissed in the house again and when I put the newspaper down to soak it up, I noticed the article. Help me up," she said, reaching for my hand.

"I just don't know what to say, Adele," I said, pulling her onto her feet. "You are getting stranger by the minute."

That's when I first began to think that I'd probably be losing her pretty soon. Here she was worried about keeping her smelly old house in West L.A. and now she'll probably be so rich that she can move to New York City or Paris, France and live in one of those fancy pre-war apartments with a view of the Left Bank and the Eiffel Tower.

When I got back home, there was an invitation in the afternoon mail with a picture of a gray haired couple in their sixties smiling like they had just won the lottery. It said, "Come to a free luncheon and lecture about Cremation."

"Want to go to a free luncheon and lecture on cremation?" I asked Adele on the phone.

"What?"

"I'm joking. I just wanted you know about the exciting new opportunities in *my* life."

That evening I sat on my sofa, thinking, which I do by crocheting hats for cancer patients who are undergoing chemo, because their heads get cold. I thought about my husband Joseph who died suddenly of a heart attack two years ago. I thought about my son Jeffrey, a high school history teacher in Torrance, who I am waiting to tell me that he is gay, although I already know it. And I thought about Adele's son Gabe, a compulsive gambler who squandered most of Adele's savings before he shot himself to death, and I thought about how grateful I was to have Jeffrey, who is a very good boy despite the sex thing. I thought about my own house, which is paid off, thank God, and the life insurance that Joseph left to cover the property taxes and homeowners insurance. And I thought about how judgmental I had been about Adele and how un-Christian that was, given my own blessed situation. I finally thought about how thirsty I was and got up off the sofa and went into the kitchen to get a glass of iced tea.

Should I have tried to loan Adele the money to pay her property tax, I wondered? Should I have just given it to her, knowing that she couldn't pay me back? I asked our minister after choir practice, and Pastor Harold told me that only God could answer those questions.

When I asked God, He referred me to Lao Tzu's proverb: "Give a man a fish and you feed him for a day. Teach a man to fish and you feed him for a lifetime." I was surprised that He quoted Lao Tzu and not the Holy Bible, but then I realized that He created Lao Tzu, too.

Lao Tzu made me think about ordering some of Suzy Orman's books on managing money for Adele to read, but I'm afraid she's too busy now getting rich and famous. By the way, I heard that Suzy Orman is gay. I guess it's no big deal anymore.

Last night I dreamed that Pastor Harold was photographing naked cherubs. I said, "Pastor, what are you doing?" and he said, "I'm photographing angels, Virginia. The Big Book of Naked Angels." "But Pastor," I said, "isn't that really kiddie porn?" He looked at me with such disappointment, as if he had offered me salvation and I had mistaken it for hell fire. I woke up in tears and I finally understood how completely I had failed Adele.

I drove over to her house and let myself in. Jefferson, her crazy old Boxer, beat his tail on the floor twice by way of greeting but didn't get up. Adele was standing on a counter in the kitchen taking empty glass jars down from the top shelf of a cabinet.

"What are you doing up there, Adele?" I asked, alarmed.

"I'm getting some jars for the kumquat marmalade I'm going to make. My little tree finally blossomed and I've got forty fat kumquats and a bag of sugar waiting to be boiled. Help me down," she said, reaching out her hand.

"Will you sit?" I asked her, because I was so full of things to tell her that I could hardly contain myself.

I told her about the angel dream and then I told her what it meant.

"God gave you a vision, Adele, and it led you out of the darkness of your tax debt by way of the light of inspiration. You knew it was completely innocent, but I made it sinful because you were clever enough to wrap it in such radiance that everyone would notice. My dear friend," I said, grasping Adele's hands and crying in shame. "I was self-righteous and afraid, while you were strong and courageous. Please forgive me."

"Oh, my goodness, Virginia, you have nothing to apologize for."

"I do, I do," I insisted.

"Let me make us a pot of tea," she said, quickly getting up and putting the kettle on the stove. She laid out two cups and a jade green pot, dropping two apple cinnamon tea bags into it. When she returned to the table, I could see that she was lost in thought.

"I don't think we need to call them *naked* angels, do you? I mean, it's a given that angels are naked, isn't it?"

"What are you talking about, Adele?"

"The book. The Big Book of Angels. We'll photograph a book of angelic children."

"No, no," I said, "it was only a dream."

"The agent is already asking me for something else. That's what they do, Virginia. When you have a best seller, they want to capitalize on it with a follow-up book."

"It was just a dream," I said, feeling a little dizzy.

"Of course this should be *our* book, Virginia, we should do it together."

"It's not a book," I said weakly, feeling swept aside by Adele's enthusiasm. "And there's probably already a Big Book of Angels."

"Well, then we'll call it The Big Book of Seraphim, the highest order of angels, or The Big Book of Cherubs. Don't worry, we'll make it work."

The kettle began to whistle but Adele ignored it until the sound grew into a scream.

"Pastor Harold should write the words for the book, don't you think?" she said, turning off the burner. "He's very learned, and esteemed. And he has the most wonderful way of making God seem easy."

Her Hair

The first thing I noticed when Jennifer walked into the waiting room that morning was her hair. She had started out with shoulder-length, straight blond hair when she began seeing me for therapy. Then the cancer hit and the chemo and she shaved her head. After she got through all that, her hair grew back white blond and she liked how it made her face stand out and decided to keep it short. But then she began to think that her hair was the reason men weren't attracted to her anymore and she started experimenting with the color. One time it turned light green and she cried for the whole therapy session. The next time it was a yellower blond. She kept that for a while and spent a whole hour talking about her hair stylist Russ and how Russ just couldn't get the color right but she didn't want to leave him because he'd been her friend for ten years.

I'm a psychoanalyst and what we do is interpret the unconscious mind of the patient in relation to *us* so I told her that maybe *I* was the "hair stylist" who couldn't get "the color" right for her and maybe she was telling me like a baby whose mommy can't find the right way to comfort her that I had to try harder and do better. But she didn't understand psychoanalytic interpretation, or care for that matter, so she said no, she wasn't talking about me or her mother but just Russ the hair stylist.

Well, sometimes psychoanalysis works and sometimes it doesn't. Anyway, this time when she came for therapy, she looked like she was wearing a faux fur wig on her head, all spiked up with gel in shades of orange, rust and yellow. Before I could get over my shock, Charlie my rooster who knew her quite well and had always behaved like a perfect gentleman before this suddenly flew up and attacked her on the legs. I had never seen anything like it before. What they do is jump in the air and aim feet first, striking out with their big sharp claws like a boxer's fists.

There wasn't any blood, thank heavens, because he didn't break the skin, but her legs were red and scratched and she was scared to death. I was pretty scared myself and grabbed Charlie and threw him into the office and yelled at him.

It took Jennifer about ten minutes to calm down. She walked all around the backyard of my house where my office was located and kept apologizing for being so upset and I kept telling her that she didn't need to apologize because it was Charlie's fault and I was incredibly sorry and I suggested that we sit outside on the deck where I had some chairs and a little fountain and we could have the session there.

So that's what we did, but the neighbor next door who usually sleeps during the day because he's a DJ on an all-night talk radio show was up and walking around outside watering his grass and even though we couldn't see him and he couldn't see us through the thick trees that grow between our properties, we could hear him and Jennifer was afraid that he could hear *her*.

But after a couple of false starts, she got into what was bothering her and it was all about her hair and how upset she was and how her friends told her she looked like a lesbian (*Some friends!* I said) and the louder she got, the quieter I was, I got so quiet she could hardly hear me and kept saying what? what? and getting irritated with me, but my instinct told me to stay quiet to help her pull herself together. Maybe my instinct was off, though, I don't know, I was pretty shaken up by the rooster attack and I began to think, in between listening to her, that it might be too much to ask patients to put up with a rooster (and a noisy Australian cockatoo, which I forgot to mention) although most of the patients didn't seem to mind, I didn't think the birds were the reason that a few other patients had quit but it was kicking the hell out of my income and I certainly didn't want to lose another one today, even though Jennifer only paid me one-third of my full fee.

She finally finished obsessing about her hair and how

unattractive she felt, and then she talked about this guy named Jeff she had asked to help her with her online cosmeceuticals business and he said sure but then he didn't follow up and she called him and emailed him and he didn't answer and she said she just knew it was because of her terrible hair and I said that Jeff's behavior didn't say anything except that she had asked the wrong person and she should look around for a better person, and that maybe she just wanted some way to explain things like rejection, which she didn't understand, and so she decided it was her fault when it wasn't at all, like apologizing to me for being upset that Charlie had attacked her when she wasn't to blame.

That made sense to her and she started to feel better and one of the last things she said was that her business was doing better and she planned to pay me more very soon, which was very good news for me after losing some patients but of course I didn't say anything about that and when she gave me twenty dollars too much for the session I gave it back to her because I wanted her to know that our relationship was not all about money.

After she left, I decided that I'd put Charlie out in the back yard when Jennifer came next time so she wouldn't have to be afraid. The only reason I didn't keep him in the back yard in the first place was because there was a law about raising chickens and all kinds of rules about 300 feet from here and 100 feet from there and the only way I could have him without getting in trouble with the animal police was to bring him inside.

So that was that, I thought, a close call and a lesson learned but disaster had been averted and I got into my sweats and went over to my computer and navigated to my emails to see what new junk I didn't want to buy or know or hear about was there and that's when I saw the email from Jennifer which said "a sad decision." She went on about how grateful she was that I got her through the cancer and the chemo and how much I had helped her and how sorry she was and how she had to find someone else who didn't have birds in the office. I wrote her a very nice reply about how sorry I was and how terrible that Charlie had attacked her and how much I had enjoyed working with her and good luck finding a new therapist and all that appropriate stuff and then I guess I went a little crazy because I said that I really had to tell her the truth about why Charlie had attacked her all of a sudden out of the blue and as much as it pained me to mention it and hoping she wouldn't take it the wrong way I said I was pretty sure that what had driven him bonkers was her hair.

The Ice Cream Cone

"Why in the world would you want an ice cream cone?" my mother demanded. It was a reasonable question, considering that we were in the middle of a freezing cold New York winter, wearing heavy coats over bulky sweaters, snug hats, wooly scarves, snow boots and, in my case, mittens.

There were seven of us at the bus stop, walking back and forth or in little circles, stomping on the hard sidewalk snow to try and keep our feet warm. I was counting out loud as I marched, "One, two, three, four, five, six, one two, three, four, five, six." A man in a brown knitted hat with a bright red face glared at me. Steam exploded out of his mouth every time he breathed. "Ooofff," he kept saying as he pounded his crossed arms against his chest. "Oooff-oooff." I giggled a little because he sounded like a dog barking.

My mother gave me a look. Her look said, "Don't bother that angry man, you're asking for trouble."

To get away from her sharp eyes, I marched over to the candy store on the corner. "Don't go too far," my mother called after me. "Jeez," my daddy would have said under his breath. "Jeez," I said. *Leave the kid alone.*

Even though we had a brand new blue and white 1953 Chevy, my daddy wouldn't drive us to grandma's house. He said New York had the best public transportation system in the country and we could damn well get to the Bronx on the bus. He said it was enough to have to drive all the way up there from the East Village to bring us home. He also said that if my mother wasn't such a scaredy-cat, we could take the subway and be there and back in no time.

But the real reason daddy wouldn't drive us to grandma's was because he and grandma hated each other. Grandma always called him "he," like "I suppose HE was too busy to drive you here."

"Don't talk that way about him in front of her," my mother would say. Daddy was the *him* and I was the *her*. But by the time my mother was vacuuming the dinner crumbs off the dark blue dining room rug, they would both say bad things about *him* in front of me.

My mother was leaning over the curb looking for the bus, so I had time to peek into the candy store. A lady in red and white stripes was making a hot fudge sundae for a man with puffy pink cheeks. She sprinkled nuts on it and then placed a cherry on top. The cherry slid down the ice cream like a sled into a pool of hot fudge. She grabbed it by the stem and put it back on top of the sundae. "Now, you stay there," she said to the cherry, as if it was a bad dog. It made me laugh. It also made me very hungry for ice cream.

"Maaaaa," I called as I was walking back to the bus stop. She hated it when I called her "Ma" but that was her name, at least to me.

"It's still not coming," she said, thinking that's what I wanted to know.

"I want an ice cream cone." You already know what she said about that. But I kept asking her anyway, and after another ten minutes she got so sick of me that she said okay.

"I just know," she said, taking a nickel from her pocketbook, "that the minute you buy the ice cream cone, the bus will come."

"No it won't," I told her, so she wouldn't change her mind.

But my mother was right. As I was coming out of the store with the ice cream cone–vanilla, my favorite flavor–she gave me the "I told you so" look and shouted, "Hurry up, the bus is coming."

The bus pulled up, scraping the curb loud like a rake, and jerked to a halt. "Hold that down low," my mother whispered, not wanting the bus driver to see the ice cream cone. The red-faced man pushed past everyone and got on first. My mother gave him a disgusted look, but he didn't care about her looks like I did.

The bus was already full. There were no seats left. Even the red-faced man had to stand. I leaned against a woman in front of me as the bus lurched forward. She was wearing a dark brown fur coat that felt as soft as peach fuzz against my cheek. My mother looked down at me and mouthed the word "mink."

I leaned my face against the fur again and yawned happily. The bus was very hot and it made the ice cream cone melt all over my mitten. My mother mouthed "Be careful." I nodded yes, but the rocking of the bus made me sleepy and I dozed off.

The next thing I remember was losing my balance and reaching my arms out to keep from falling. The ice cream plunged deep into the fur of the lady's mink coat with the cone sticking straight out. It looked like a little white-faced organ grinder monkey with a clown's hat on its head.

My mother gasped in horror. I hadn't seen her look that upset since I was three and flushed her ruby bracelet down the toilet. She put a finger up to her lips to say "quiet!" and grabbed me hard by the shoulder, pushing me as fast as she could toward the front of the bus. I got one last look at my poor ice cream cone before she yanked me down the bus steps and back out onto the street.

She was so angry at me that she talked to God. "Have you ever seen anything like that in your life?" she asked Him, looking up at the dark gray sky. God must have agreed with her because when her eyes came back down from heaven, she gave me a "you are the most aggravating child in the whole world" look.

It was the only thing she could talk about at grandma's house until grandma said it was her fault for buying me an ice cream cone in the first place. That made my mother cry.

"Why don't you ever take my side?" she asked grandma, burying her face in a handful of Kleenex. Then grandma said it was really HIS fault for not driving us on such a cold day.

That night after daddy came to pick us up, my mother told him how angry she was at grandma for saying mean things to her. But when he agreed that grandma was an old witch, she said that grandma wouldn't have talked to her that way if she'd married a better man.

I felt sad for daddy, who hadn't done anything wrong. It was really *my* fault for asking to have an ice cream cone before we got on the bus, but I didn't know until right then that a little thing like an ice cream cone can wreck your whole family.

"Maybe if you give mommy a mink coat," I told him, trying to make things better, "she won't be mad at you anymore, and even grandma will like you."

But I guess my mother didn't like that idea very much because she twisted around to me in the back seat with a really mean look and told me to shut up and go to sleep.

Psyche and Eros

I overhear Pedilla telling Ramirez there are bedbugs in his house and I tell him, Pedilla, you can't come to school with bedbugs, they'll get into your clothes and your book bag and the other kids'll bring them home with them and we'll have a bedbug epidemic.

What'm I suppose to do, Mr. O'Brien? he whines, my parents ain't gonna listen to me.

They gotta do something, I say. It's my responsibility to report Pedilla to the principal and Aramanian sure as shit'll kick him out and won't let him come back until the bugs are gone.

So I report it and sure enough Aramanian kicks Pedilla out and his mother calls me on the phone and cries *!dios mio* and *!que lio* and *!que lastimo* and I can't say much to calm her because my Spanish is lousy and what can I do anyway, I'm just a Cesar Chavez High School history teacher who wishes he was Ken Burns.

So Pedilla is out for two weeks, which certainly won't do his American History grade any good, and when he comes back, he shows me some kind of bill or invoice or something that says Santos Psychic Pest Control and some scratchy looking handwriting I can't exactly read and then $78 near the bottom.

Psychic Pest Control? I say, halfway between a laugh and a scoff, and Pedilla says, Man, I swear, them bugs is as gone as free tacos at a church picnic.

Nicely put, I say. You talk to Mr. Aramanian yet? And he says, Yeah, I showed him the bill and he said hmmmmph.

Hmmmmmph? I repeat.

That's what he said, Mr. O'Brien, I swear.

That afternoon I go pick up my mail from the office and then stick my head into Aramanian's office.

Psychic Pest Control? I say with a big grin on my face.

I called 'em, he says. Spoke to Santos's daughter. She said Santos was out on an *infestation,* that's what she said, an *infestation!* like she's a snooty college girl or something. So I say, what exactly is psychic pest control? Come around some morning, early, she says, and her mother'll show me.

Her *mother?*

I guess Santos is *Mrs*. Santos.

Are you gonna?

Am I gonna what?

Are you gonna go?

I don't know. I haven't made up my mind, he says.

Pedilla said those bugs were gone faster than free tacos at a church picnic.

Nice turn of phrase, Aramanian says.

Yeah, he can get it together when he wants to.

Wanna come with me, Burt? Maybe she'll do your horrorscope.

Who's gonna teach my first period class? I say, glad to have an excuse.

Mrs. Hoover'll cover for you, he says, the bastard. Hoover's the school floater.

Two mornings later, Aramanian puts on one of his less dingy white shirts with his old gray herringbone jacket and the maroon paisley tie, the only one he owns without gravy stains. He picks me up at 6:30 a.m., Nancy isn't even awake yet, and we go over to meet Mrs. Pest Control Psychic.

I assume we're going somewhere like a business, you know, Western Exterminator or Terminix, but it's just a regular house, kind of a rundown Craftsman, with a hand-painted little sign on the lawn, Santos Psychic Pest Control. For some reason I get the chuckles, the whole thing's making me a little nervous to be honest.

So there she is, Mrs. Domenica Santos, making breakfast for her daughter Marisa, who looks to be about thirteen, and they've both got these huge dark eyes, spooky eyes like in *Night of the Living Dead* or *Nightmare on Elm Street*, but they're still pretty in a Hispanic sort of way, striking I guess you'd say. Anyway, the first thing Aramanian does is bump into the kitchen table like Joe Spazz and he nearly knocks over Marisa's orange juice glass when he reaches for the cup of coffee Mrs. Santos offers him.

She looks at him with those spooky eyes and says, When did your wife die?

Aramanian almost drops the coffee cup. His hand starts to shake.

Then she looks over at me and says, Shame on you.

I wanna get the hell out of there, but Aramanian looks like he's ready to move in and marry her, and he's my ride.

Okay, I had a little, shall we say, unauthorized activity with Miss Kolchak, the social studies intern, it was nothing much, just a couple of times last spring when Nancy was in Tucson helping her mother with a broken hip. But who does this woman who's not even my wife think she is, saying *shame on you* like she's the Mexican Morality Mafia or something.

Aramanian looks over at me with one of his hairy eyebrows raised so high I think it's going to break in half and fall off his face.

So what about showing us how you get rid of bugs, I say to her, not even trying to hide how pissed off I am.

She looks at me like I'm one of the bugs she wants to eradicate and says, I don't have no insects here, mister. Then she turns to Aramanian and says, You come back without him and I'll show you. It don't work with non-believers, their negativity messes up the *hechizo*.

Then she looks over at me and says, the *juju,* like I'm an ignoramus or something.

On the way back to school, Aramanian says, You behaving badly, Burt?

Yeah, I say, I'm messing with Ariel Hutchinson's *juju*.

Ariel Hutchinson is a 200 pound lesbian who teaches women's studies and p.e.

Watch yourself, Aramanian says.

Watch your own self, Sargise, I say. That lady has her eye on you.

What happens next I have to tell you second hand because I wasn't going to get within a mile of that creepy psychic lady again. You can probably guess anyway, because Aramanian was a widower who hadn't had any action for three years and Domenica Santos woke up his sex drive like a Mt. Kiluea eruption. You could practically see black steam pouring out of both his hairy ears.

I'm a goner, he tells me one afternoon as we're walking out to our cars. Not that I want to get away from Domenica or anything. It's just that–can I speak frankly?

Sure.

I never knew what–he whispers the word *sex*–was like, you know what I mean?

Your wife wouldn't put out?

No, she put out. Kind of. She didn't know any better than I did. Armenians, what can I say. But Domenica, oh my God, you know what I mean?

Yeah. I'm familiar with Oh my God.

You and Nancy, huh?

On a good day.

So Aramanian was gob-smacked, or as my college roommate Bruce at UC San Diego delicately put it, *fuck struck*. He used to say, a man who is fuck struck might just as well lay his neck down on the block and wait for the chopper.

So that's when the trouble begins. Because apparently Armenians don't like Mexicans, and Aramanian's family isn't too cordial to Mrs. Santos when Sargise brings her to their restaurant.

They keep speaking to me in Armenian, he says, and she keeps speaking to me in Spanish and they want to know what she's saying and she wants to know what they're saying and eventually she says, *Ibasta!* Get me outta here! Then she cries all night long and keeps saying, They don't think I'm good enough for you!

So here's poor fuck struck Sargise Aramanian, caught between his family and his passion, and while some other guy might just say, fuck it, passion trumps family, Aramanian is Armenian and family is a big deal for them.

You're killing me, Aramanian says to Domenica.

No! You're killing *me*! she fires back. If they really love you, they should love me.

One afternoon I come into the office and Aramanian is collapsed face down on his desk with his curly salt and pepper hair spread out on the blotter like someone snuck up and clubbed him in the back of his head.

Jesus, Sargise! Are you okay?

He looks up at me with bloodshot eyes and puffy red cheeks and you won't believe what he tells me.

She put a hex on my family, he says, wringing his hands like they're holding some animal he's trying to strangle the life out of.

What?

She sent cockroaches to their restaurant, Burt! *Ashtarak*, Zagat's Best Armenian Food in Los Angeles, "A" rating ten years in a row. Oh my God. It turns out she doesn't just make bugs scram. She can send them wherever she wants them to go.

Jesus, I say, realizing what a close call I had with her that first day and didn't even know it. This is not a lady you want to piss off.

I begged her, Aramanian says, make the roaches go away, and she says, only if I turn my back on my family and choose her instead.

What are you going to do? I ask. The whole situation is giving me the creeps to be honest, like she could decide any minute to send a plague to the school.

I called an exterminator, Aramanian says.

You're going to have her killed? I whisper.

No, no, for the roaches.

Sargise, you've got to make up with her, I say a little breathlessly. What if she sends frogs to the school, or rats? Kills our first born? Who knows? She's crazy.

Yes, but very powerful. She won't even tell me what happened to *Mr.* Santos. He was unfaithful to her and then he disappeared. Gone since seven years ago. Nobody can find him.

What are you going to do?

Marry her.

You're going to marry her?

What else can I do?

You're right, I say, relieved, even though it feels like I'm pushing him off a cliff. The poor sap, she has his huevos in her fists and now we're all at risk.

You've got to take one for the team, I say, that's all there is to it.

Will you please come with me to my family's restaurant tonight, Burt? I've got to try to talk to them and they won't hurt me if you're there.

Hurt you? What are they, the Mob?

Worse.

So I tell Nancy that Sargise needs a body guard and around five the two of us head over to Ashtarak, which Sargise says means *fortress*.

The food is wonderful, he says as we're driving, have you ever had Armenian food?

What about the bugs? I ask, although my real worry is whether Armenians carry guns.

Gone, he says, but my auntie still won't speak to me. She called me *kapikee vor*.

What does that mean?

Monkey's ass, he whispers, making a right into the mini-mall on Santa Monica Blvd. and parking his big black Cadillac sedan.

Go ahead of me, he says, pushing me through the double

doors of the restaurant, which takes up practically the whole mall, except for a Supercuts.

I see what looks like *The Family* back near the kitchen: an old man with thick glasses sitting next to the deli section with a plate of something brown, another man behind the bar in shirt sleeves with salt and pepper hair like Sargise, and a stout woman in her seventies wearing an apron over her dress with big orange flowers and one of those old fashioned beauty parlor hair-dos with tight curls that looks like a wig. Their cheery smiles freeze as soon as they see Sargise behind me. I look around for weapons.

Barev, tanti Hranoush, Sargise says, or something that sounds like that. This is my friend from school, Burt O'Brien. He teaches history.

Sargise is holding me in front of himself like a shield.

I told Burt that Ashtarak has the finest Armenian food in Los Angeles, he says, desperate to recover their favor.

In all of America, the old man corrects, his voice a gruff gargle.

Barev, Uncle Guregh. I see you are enjoying the delicious Moujadara. May we join you?

Before the old guy can answer, Sargise steers me to a table near him and we sit.

What should we order tonight, Tanti, he says, shaking out a napkin for me as if I am a ten-year-old boy. If he tries to cut my food, I swear I'll punch him in the head.

The old lady comes over to me and puts her hand on my shoulder.

Is this your first Armenian meal? she asks in a sugary voice, like I am her favorite nephew.

Yes, Tanti, Sargise says.

Did you hear someone speak? she asks me with a mischievous smile. It must be ghosts, she says. Some dead man's ghost.

Tanti, Sargise pleads, I am here to apologize to you. Please open your heart.

Let me get you a menu, she says, as if I have come there alone.

Just then, a family of five crashes through the double doors, the kids in a squabble that must have started back in the car.

Shut up, the eight-year-old says to his sister. She tries to kick him in the leg but he twists like a pretzel out of her reach.

Arman! Kohar! the old lady says and then something like "par-ee your eggo," clapping her hands together in greeting.

Sargise slumps in his chair like a deflated tire. She will never forgive me, he mumbles.

The man behind the bar comes over to our table with two glasses of red wine. I'm hoping for Sargise's sake that it's a gesture of mercy.

He whispers something like "peanut shoon cockney."

Sargise groans.

What did he say? I ask, guessing that it wasn't *we all love you.*

I don't want to say, Sargise whispers, twisting his napkin into a damp ball. I can't say it.

Yes you can. Tell me.

He said *the dog should shit on him*, the old man shouts.

Ah, those crazy Armenians.

It's a nice enough church wedding, modest but appropriately festive for a second marriage between two weird middle-aged people. The bride wears a rose-colored dress and a wreath of white lilies of the valley in her pinned-up hair and Aramanian looks almost dapper in his clean white shirt and rented tux. The church is full of Domenica's family–cousins, aunts and uncles, Domenica's mother and her daughter Marisa, and a couple dozen other Mexican children in their Sunday school clothes.

Aramanian's family is conspicuously absent, but he has begged all the Chavez teachers to come in their place, and most of us have taken pity on him so we're here bearing witness.

Nancy and I have brought the couple a Wolfgang Puck pressure cooker as a wedding gift, the expensive model because we don't want to give the next Mrs. Aramanian any reason to resent us. The table for presents is stacked high with other big boxes in fancy wrapping, so we're obviously not the only ones who are hedging our bets.

After the ceremony, which thank God is short, we go outside to the church's back lawn where the reception is being held. I grab a Dos Equis from the ice chest, feeling a little nervous that Domenica will decide to say something to Nancy about me diddling the intern. But she is being nice as pie.

Sargise, she says, her arm wrapped around the groom's sucked-in waist, make them come to dinner soon. Tell them about my delicious calda de mariscos.

Aramanian, who was a little drunk even before the ceremony, gives her a slobbering kiss on the cheek.

She channeled Elvis this morning, he says proudly. He sent us his very best wishes.

I want to say, Drinking the Kool-Aid, eh, Sargise? But not with her standing right next to him with those spooky eyes.

She seems very sweet, Nancy says to me when we're out of earshot. Nancy could look at Satan and see Mother Theresa.

You're just lucky she didn't turn me into a cockroach, I say, tickled by my wife's tender heart.

When Nancy goes off to the ladies room, I check out the buffet table, decked out with platters of fresh fruit and vegetables and trays of chicharron, tamales, roasted chicken, and albondigas. Lopez, the ESL teacher whose beer gut's spilling over his belt loops like muffin mix, is loading up his plate.

Hey, Burt, dig in, he says, not wanting to be the only one pigging out, I guess.

Hot enough for you, he says, and I notice that the underarms of his light green shirt are soaked with perspiration. But look, no bugs, he says, waving his plate around recklessly. Not one fly.

The wife is in psychic pest control, I say, reaching for a plate.

Wonder if she could get rid of my *chingaso* brother-in-law, he says with a laugh, nudging a tamale over with his fat index finger to make room for a hefty chicken breast.

I pop a quartet of small meatballs into my mouth, stoked by the idea of Domenica turning someone other than me into a toad. I feel kind of relieved, like I've just made an illegal u-turn and the cop didn't spot me.

There's a sharp poke in my right kidney.

I love your wife, she says.

Me, too, I say, turning toward Domenica, my words mixed with ground pork.

I love Nancy, she says again, leaning so close I can feel her warm breath in my ear. Her dark eyes burn two holes in my face.

Got it, I say, feeling like she's waiting for me to reach into my pants and hand her my stones.

We're all going to be so happy, she says with an explosive laugh, clapping her hands together like a televangelist.

'Til death us do part, I mumble, the half-eaten meatballs threatening to choke me before they go down.

That's when it dawns on me what that wedding ceremony was really all about. I finally get the big picture, as they say, like those out-of-focus times in the eye doctor's office when he snaps in the corrective lenses and suddenly you can read the last line of letters on the eye chart.

H-o-l-y-s-h-i-t.

Sargise Aramanian was not the only guy who received a life sentence today.

TALL

For as long as she could remember, Tookie Basch wanted to be tall, like one of those willowy teenagers with legs and necks like giraffes in *Vogue* and *Mademoiselle*. And one Monday morning in April, after a long night of vodka martinis and shameless flirtation with the keyboard player in the band at her married sister's 40th birthday party, Tookie woke up seven feet tall.

She was, admittedly, very hung over but that could not account for why the blond oak floor was two extra feet from her eyes when she looked down. Or that her feet would no longer fit into her Fuzzy Froggy bedroom slippers.

She walked barefoot to the full length mirror across from the bed but she could only see herself from the waist down. She had to move backwards, banging her head as she passed through the doorway into the hall, to get the whole picture and when she did, she cried out in shock.

"Oh my God!"

Her husband Dan woke up long enough to shout, "What?" but when he saw through half-shut, myopic eyes that she was neither hanging from the ceiling fan nor lying naked and bloody from knife wounds, he promptly fell back to sleep.

This reassured Tookie until she remembered that her husband had stopped noticing anything about her a couple of years earlier.

Born Karen Basch thirty-six years ago, her mother called her Cookie, which her four-year-old sister Monica pronounced "Tookie," and Tookie stuck. Monica was tall like her mother and father, five foot eight by the time she reached fourteen, but Tookie was a runt, stopping her climb toward stature at a diminutive five foot three.

Tookie sat back down on her side of the bed and began to cry, her enlarged hands laying palms up in her lap like halibut fillets.

"Oh my, oh my," she said.

Dan mumbled something about coffee and then reached over to the night table, first for his glasses and then for the clock to see if he could steal a few more minutes of sleep. He didn't have to be at Deloitte and Touche, where he was a Senior Accountant, until 9:20.

"Dan? Danny? Could you turn over and take a look at

me?"

Her husband rolled over without curiosity and faced his wife's hunched-over back.

"What?"

She stood up and turned around to face him, her pale green nightgown barely reaching her meatless thighs. Her arms had lengthened toward her knees, which now looked knobby, and her legs, once thick with muscle from thousands of miles on the treadmill, had stretched into slender ropes.

"Holy shit."

They sat in Dr. Blechner's waiting room without an appointment because this was an emergency, Dan insisted, and they damn well needed some answers.

Dr. Blechner didn't have any.

"Good heavens," he said when he saw this woman he'd known for more than a decade. Tookie was wearing a pair of her husband's trousers that looked on her like capri pants and a red plaid flannel shirt with unbuttoned sleeves that barely surpassed her elbows. The doctor checked Tookie's heart and lungs, took a urine sample, and then drew blood, shaking his head several times in the process as if shaking would jostle the situation into perspective.

"Have you ever seen anything like this before, Doctor?" Dan asked.

"Well . . ." Dr. Blechner said, pulling on one of his earlobes, "I've seen pictures of acromegaly in the textbooks. But I don't think this is acromegaly."

"Am I going to die?" Tookie asked, trying not to cry. She felt sure her condition was fatal.

"No, no," Dr. Blechner said reassuringly, but in truth he didn't have the slightest idea.

For the first time since their marriage six years earlier, Dan went clothes shopping with his wife.

"You can't go around wearing my clothes," he said. "They look ridiculous and they don't even fit."

"I'm sorry," Tookie said as if she'd backed the car into their garbage cans or shrunk his favorite sweater.

He should have said it wasn't her fault but he wasn't convinced that was true. *She must have done something wrong*, he thought, but he just couldn't imagine what.

After Dan dropped Tookie off at home, hurrying downtown to his office in the Chicago Loop, she floated around their Sheridan Road condo like a stranger who'd wandered into someone else's life. Feeling a little dizzy, perhaps from the altitude, Tookie sat down in the breakfast nook with her coffee and peanut buttered bagel and stared at her iphone in the charger. She felt that she should call somebody but she could not think of what to say. *Oh, hi, Mom, guess what? I just grew two feet last night while I was sleeping.* She knew better than to give an hysteric like her mother a reason to become hysterical, and this was a really good reason. Of course, she would eventually have to tell her family. But now that Monica's 40th birthday had been put to rest, she didn't expect to see them for a while, which was fine with her.

Tookie decided to call her friend Wanda. Bizarre as it sounds, Wanda had been abducted by aliens from the Leda 25177 galaxy in the Hydra Supercluster when she was a pimply-faced teenager. They returned her to earth with clear skin and the formula for a spongy white mud that cured acne, which her parents subsequently sold to Merle Norman for a very large undisclosed amount. Tookie felt sure that Wanda, who thanks to the abduction was now independently wealthy, would know how to put Tookie's transformation in perspective.

"When I woke up this morning, I was seven feet tall," Tookie said when Wanda answered.

"Are you at work?"

"No. I called in sick." Tookie usually called Wanda from her office at Leo Burnett, where she was an advertising media buyer.

"Are you sick?"

"No, but I'm seven feet tall, Wanda. Actually six foot eleven and a fourth. The doctor measured me."

"You went to see the doctor?"

"Dan thought a doctor would know what was going on."

"Did he know?"

"No, he wasn't sure."

"It's God's mysterious will," Wanda said, which was what she always said when strange things happened.

"Dan had to buy me a bunch of new clothes. He went with me to Marshall Field's."

"Well, that's good," Wanda said. "They have a lot of nice things at Fields."

For the rest of the day, Tookie explored the upper half of the condominium. She replaced the burned out bulbs in the dining room chandelier, the track lights in the living room, and the carriage lamp in the entryway. She dusted the tops of the bookcases, which had not been touched since she and Dan moved in. She pruned and watered the hanging plants on the balcony, and she tackled the floor to ceiling windows with vinegar and newspaper.

Then she went outside and took a walk. She touched the soft, moist leaf buds that were opening on the oak tree branches, peeked into a robin's nest and counted three spotted blue eggs, and observed that most of the neighboring rain gutters were clogged with winter debris. She also discovered that she scared small dogs and startled old women, most of whom could only make eye contact with her navel. And every so often, if she stood on her toes, she caught a glimpse of the silver gray waters of Lake Michigan. Tookie began to think that short people were as tragically handicapped as the deaf and blind, and imagined organizing a fundraiser to promote compassion and understanding for the vertically challenged. Waking up tall, she thought, was certainly not the worst thing that could happen to a person.

That night, Tookie put on the new black extra-long Marshall Fields nightie that Dan had bought her and for the first time in six years tried to initiate their lovemaking.

"I'm a different woman now, Danny. Don't you think we should re-consummate our marriage?"

"I don't know," Dan said, shying away from her. At five foot nine, he barely came to the top of her chest. "You feel like a stranger to me, Took, I can't help it."

"I thought men liked new women," she said.

"Not this new," Dan said.

"Well, it's not new down there," she said.

"How do you know?" he said. "Everything else is different."

"Not my breasts," she said.

"That's true," Dan agreed sadly.

"You're such a shit," Tookie said, surprising herself with the exclamation, and she wanted to say even more. But instead she just crawled into the bed, which was now a foot too short for her legs, and wept.

Tookie woke up very early the next morning and got into the office at 7:30. After Dan's reaction the night before, she was determined to avoid attention. But when *The Morning Show* caterer went past her office in the hallway at 9:30, Tookie called to her, hoping that if she stayed seated, the girl wouldn't notice her height. Tookie craved something sweet like a cinnamon bun or a maple bar and now that she was as tall as a Chicago Bulls shooting guard, she could eat anything she wanted without worrying about getting fat. It would have been great if only her height weren't quite so extreme. Six feet would have been plenty, she thought, but her predicament was like Alice and the eat-me pills.

Almost the same thing had happened to Tookie when she was twelve and wished for breasts. She went from nothing to a C-cup practically overnight, and got teased for being "chesty." Then she lost *too* much of it when she was on Weight Watchers in her twenties, and never got it back. You had to be careful what you wished for, she thought, making a mental note.

Fortunately, the lunch date she'd scheduled was with a new client, NaturalCat Organic Cat Food, so he wouldn't look shocked when she met him at the restaurant. She spent all morning tweaking her media plan, carefully addressing the changes her boss Luther had requested to beef up the organic-only pubs. She stopped only long enough to learn that all her medical tests had come back normal and to respond to Wanda's text message urging her to contact Oprah or Dr. Oz.

At noon, Tookie left the agency by a side door, feeling relieved that she'd survived the morning without being outed.

Evan Collier was waiting for her at the bar when she arrived at The Gage, one of the trendy new downtown lunch venues. She was relieved to see that his cocktail was a Perrier with lime, because her last Cat client had been a raging alcoholic. Better still, Collier was tall, over six feet two, she estimated, although he only came up to her chin.

"Delighted to meet you," he said, grasping her hand and looking her over like she was a brand new Maserati. He had the kind of man's face that usually came with a dusty Stetson and a big open sky. Tookie had been stooping a little when she approached him, but his smile made her stand up straight.

How she ended up at the Hotel Sofitel Water Tower that afternoon, wrapped in Evan Collier's burly arms, she could not explain – although the two apple martinis she downed probably smoothed the way. She had not only betrayed her husband, she had violated a cardinal rule of business. Of course, she knew that plenty of people, including her boss Luther, violated that rule, but it was so unlike Tookie. What was it about being tall that had changed her so profoundly? And the worst of it was that she wasn't even sorry. She hadn't let herself realize until today how neglected she'd felt, how unnoticed and unappreciated by Dan. This man, Evan Collier, had made love to her like she was a gorgeous, sensual gazelle, delighting in her long limbs and soft skin and sweet taste. No, she definitely was not sorry. And if he asked her to join him for another romantic rendezvous, or even a runaway weekend in Belize, she just might say yes, and yes, and yes.

When Tookie returned to Leo Burnett late that afternoon, she no longer tried to hide. She strode through the lobby with a big smile on her face and laughed with enjoyment when the receptionist gaped at her. *Get used to it,* she thought.

"What the hell *happened* to you?" her boss Luther said when she came into his office. "You look like a goddam flamingo!"

"I had a growth spurt," she said, and sat down in his love seat, crossing her legs in the becoming manner that only tall, skinny women execute properly. "By the way, the lunch went well. Evan signed off on the media plan without any changes."

"Really? I heard he was a sonovabitch," Luther said, holding his stubbly jowls in the cup of his hand.

"Not to me," Tookie said, smiling provocatively. She knew Luther wouldn't believe what she'd been up to that afternoon even if she showed him a videotape, but it was fun to tease him a little.

"What the hell happened to *you*?" he said again with a low, soft whistle.

That night, after Tookie slid under the covers with her husband, she said, "we'll have to get a bigger bed, honey."

"Maybe you'll wake up tomorrow and be short again," Dan said, continuing to read the latest Alex Cross mystery. He seemed to have lost interest in his wife's predicament once Dr. Blechner couldn't diagnose it.

"I wouldn't count on it," Tookie said, although the thought made her a little anxious.

"Well, we'll just have to make the best of it," he said, which was Dan's way of telling her he had stopped listening.

Later that night, Tookie's cold toes woke her up and she went into the kitchen to make herself a cup of herbal tea. She augmented it with a slice of red velvet birthday cake left over from her sister Monica's party, scraping the remnants of cream cheese frosting off the plate with her fork.

In the soft light of the kitchen dimmers, she examined her legs and arms, stretching them out to their full lengths and taking deep, relaxing breaths. *Goddam flamingo!* she thought, smiling at the recollection. She realized that this bizarre transformation had given her more than height. It had given her perspective, enabled her to–what was that expression?–to see the forest for the trees. And she knew that even if she woke up five foot three again tomorrow morning, she would not be the same woman she used to be. She intended to ask more of Dan, to insist that he rise to her occasion. She would no longer mouse around like a timid housemaid, or let him treat her like a footstool he only noticed when he tripped over it.

The stove clock said 2:10, but she did not feel pressured to return to bed. She savored all the tiny sounds that punctuated the night's silence, the refrigerator motor, the ice maker, a window's hoarse rattle as a car sped past outside, even the soft click of the clock hand to 2:11.

Tookie decided that her friend Wanda was right. Whatever happened, it was God's mysterious will. *Somebody's* mysterious will at any rate, she thought, embracing the mystery without fear. And while it meant that some poor soul in Prague might wake up one morning as a cockroach, on a different morning a hundred years later, a short woman in Chicago could just as well wake up tall.

Exhibition Eater

I grew up in a family that worshipped God in the temple, but food at home. They were scandalized when a cousin by marriage, a heathen named Marlene, laid out five slices of cheese for four people and concluded, when they were too polite to take the last slice, that she had served too much.

This same Marlene invited my parents and me to dinner and set out four small bowls of soup. That was it! Soup! And it wasn't a thick soup with lots of chicken or beef and dumplings. It was more like a broth. We sat at the table drumming our fingers and waiting for the next course for almost an hour until Marlene served dessert. Five cookies, and they weren't even chocolate chip, just some stale gingersnaps which tasted like dog kibble. Marlene finally ate the fifth one so we didn't have to worry about being impolite.

But even though the adults in my family were food worshippers (with the exception of Marlene), my kid cousins were finicky eaters. They liked their hotdogs with *ketchup*! And they thought mustard, even the yellow French's kind, was the condiment of death. And if anybody tried to force something like *chopped liver* on them, they'd hide under the table or retch their way to the bathroom with a chorus of euus, arrrghs, ughhs, and brfffs.

I, on the other hand, *loved* chopped liver. I even liked *raw oysters* (so long as they were loaded with cocktail sauce). That's how I became the family's exhibition eater, starting when I was four.

"Look at Jamie. She eats everything!" That's what they'd tell their kids, which didn't exactly endear me to my cousins, who thought I was just showing off.

I also liked bones. Give me a bone and I was busy for an hour, especially if it was a lamb leg bone, or a roast beef bone, or a Porterhouse steak bone, although I could polish off one of those in half the time. I also liked chicken bones, which I cracked open with my teeth so I could suck out the marrow.

"I hope you won't do that in a restaurant, or when you go out on a date, Jamie," my dad would say, although at the age of four, I thought it was a moot point.

But I knew he was proud of the way I ate because it was a status symbol in our family to have a kid like me and he didn't have a lot of status at the time, being a mostly- unemployed musician. It was also something we had in common, like garlic or Worcestershire sauce, or roast duck, which was my absolute favorite.

You might be inclined to think that I was a fat kid, but judging from pictures, I was skinny until I became eight. At eight, I had a little belly and my cheeks were on the chubby side. That was around the time my parents got divorced, so I guess food became a consolation.

When I was in high school, I baked a devil's food cake with chocolate whipped cream icing and polished off the whole thing in less than two days. And once, when I was babysitting, I ate an entire canned ham, jelly and all, even though after the first few bites, it tasted like a salt lick. I remember hiding the can deep in the family's garbage pail so they wouldn't know what I'd done until they went looking for the ham, probably a long time later, I figured, and by then they wouldn't suspect me.

But in my senior year of high school, I decided I wanted to be popular so I bleached my brown hair platinum blond and went on a diet. The boy I had my eye on was a sexy Italian guy named Joe Agozino who played pretend bongos on the school desks, and Joe liked skinny blonds. Once I became a skinny blond, sure enough, Joe liked me. And he didn't even seem to mind that I was a *smart* blond instead of a dumb one. He became my obsession and I could hardly stand to eat. You could have waved a prime rib or a roast duck at me back then and I wouldn't have even blinked. All I wanted was Joe.

"How come you like me so much?" he'd ask.

"Because you're wonderful."

"What's so wonderful about me?"

"Everything."

"How come you won't let me French kiss you, then?"

That's where our relationship got rocky. According to Joe, all the *dumb* blonds French kissed.

This was a long time ago, when French kissing was *verboten*, not like now, when "oral" isn't even considered sex. This was when girls who "went all the way" were called "tramps." Not that French kissing was "all the way." But it was definitely *on* the way, and at the time it seemed to me like a slippery slope.

So Joe and I broke up. And that's when I started to eat again. There was a big empty space in me that Joe had filled, and food was the only other way I knew how to handle it. Joe was my first *badass*, although back then we called them *hoods*, short for hoodlum. But he wasn't really a *hood*, just a sweet, horny teenager who joined the Army after he graduated from high school and was killed in a helicopter crash on his way to Hanau Army Airfield in Hessen, Germany. After I heard about that, I was really sorry that I hadn't French kissed him. I hope a whole lot of other girls did.

That summer, I made a lot of secret trips in my mother's Chevrolet to the Donut Depot, pretending for the counter boy's benefit that there were several other people out in the car waiting for doughnuts.

"Okay, Jane wants two glazed, and Henry wants an old fashioned and a maple bar. Let me see, I think Terry said he wanted a bear claw, and Tony definitely asked for two chocolate-with-sprinkles. How many is that? Seven? Okay then, just give me two chocolate bars, an apple fritter, and... two glazed twists."

Back in the car, I'd eat the whole dozen and they wouldn't even fill me up. Food can get tricky when you start eating for all the wrong reasons.

At college, I got skinny again because the cafeteria food at the dorm was grotty, and there was this boy–Dolph.

"Is that short for Dolphin?

"No, Adolph."

"As in Hitler?"

"He spelled it differently."

I didn't have the heart to correct him.

Dolph was a tall, blond, sun-bronzed surfer boy from Malibu, Calfornia and just walking next to him made me feel proud. So I went on the black coffee diet, like ten or twelve cups a day, and got really skinny. We did just great with each other for a couple of weeks, rolling around on his bed in the fraternity house kissing and *almost* "doing it." But then we completely ran out of anything to say to each other. I mean like nothing, not one word. So I had to admit to myself that the most beautiful boy in the world was totally boring. And that, as they say, was that.

My weight continued to go the way of my love life, up when I was unattached, down when I had a beau. In New York, after I graduated from college, I had my first major relationship, with a crazy minimalist painter named Georg who made me so insecure, I became anorexic.

"You see that boat, Jamie? That's how I'm going to leave you," he'd say.

"Don't say that, Georg. You're making me cry."

"You see that girl, the pretty one in the halter top with the blond ponytail? That's who I'm going to leave you for."

"Georg, stop! Do you want me to kill myself?"

He got up to 200 pounds during the three years we were together and I dropped down to 89, living on chocolate bars, malted milk and a steak every three or four days at Max's Kansas City, which I had to split with Georg because we were poor. I wrote down every detail of our tortured relationship in tiny printed letters like a medieval monk's manuscript, three journals' worth, until the last entry said, "I am pregnant."

For the next nine months I ate enormous breakfasts of bacon and eggs and toast dripping with butter, and lots of cold milk. And for dinner I had a huge carton of pork fried rice from one of the best Sechuan restaurants in Chinatown. Still, I only weighed 104 pounds the day after I gave birth.

Georg was amazed that he had made a baby and he tried to be a good father but it just wasn't in him. He eventually left me and Gunther for a sculptor who made plaster knots that looked like elephant snot.

My weight has been up and down since then, except for the time when my vodka and Chardonnay diet took me way up and kept me there for most of a decade. But lately, after losing 25 pounds, I've become the exhibition eater for Weightwatchers.

"Look here," I say, mixing a small amount of yogurt and dill dressing into a baby kale salad with a four ounce side of water-packed canned salmon. "A delicious, filling, vegetable and protein lunch that's only six points out of the 30-point daily allowance."

And there isn't even a man in my life as an incentive, I'm proud to say, although I always keep my eye out for one.

He Had a Hat

In my experience, Catholics invariably treat God with respect. But Jews, a lot of them, act like God is a rich, blustering relative who's chronically late to holiday dinners and is often unavailable when you need his help. There is a long, proud history of disgruntled Jews–Job, Jesus, Phillip Roth, Larry Kramer. And of course, Woody Allen. Woody has been quoted as saying, "If God exists, the best you can say about him is that he's an underachiever."

My favorite Jewish joke perfectly captures that contentious spirit. A Jewish woman named Esther is well into her forties when she finally conceives, and gives birth to a son whom she worships like the second coming of you-should-excuse-the-expression Christ. One day when she and the little boy are sitting on a beach building a sand castle, a gigantic wave rises out of the ocean, crashes onto the shore and sweeps the little boy out to sea. The distraught mother jumps to her feet, looks up at heaven and cries out at the top of her lungs, "God! You made me wait half a lifetime to give birth to my beloved son and now you have the nerve to take him back? Listen to me, *ha-shem*, you bring that boy back right this minute, do you hear me?" A moment later, another giant wave rises up out of the ocean and crashes onto the sand, laying the boy back at his mother's feet. Esther looks down at her son and then back up to heaven.

"He had a hat."

Now, that's funny in a way that is particularly Jewish. Because Jews are Olympic Champion complainers–*kvetchers* in Yiddish–who can find fault with even the most positive outcomes. Let's say someone gives you a Ralph Lauren pocketbook. Did it have to be *brown*? You win the Academy Award for Best Picture. Couldn't it have happened last year when your father was still alive?

It is no accident that Freud was a Jew, because who else would know more about civilization's discontents? We Jews have the therapy gene. I myself am a psychoanalyst. And I have had my share of *mishegas*. But that's how it should be. If you are a fish, *gefilte* or otherwise, with a problem and I am a fish without problems, how am I going to understand your problem?

Enough said.

My cousin Estelle, my only living relative in Los Angeles, may she live a long and painful life, sent me a postcard announcing that she and her husband Jeremy, both Ph.D.s in psychology, were opening a new practice in therapeutic mediation. It just so happened that I had a patient, a high functioning lunatic named Wilmot, who had a low functioning lunatic brother named Sturgis, and the brother was driving my patient even crazier than he already was. I thought, "Perfect!" If anyone needed therapeutic mediation, it was those brothers, so I gave them my cousin's name and number, not of course mentioning that she was a relative.

Two weeks later, I received a phone call around 9:30 at night and an unfamiliar voice said, "Eleanor?"

Nobody has called me Eleanor since I changed my name to Veronica at 15, nobody, that is, except my cousin Estelle. Even my parents called me Veronica and wrote their letters to Veronica, and left their life insurance policies to Veronica when they died.

"Who is this?" I asked cautiously.

"It's Sturgis, Wilmot's brother."

"How can I help you, Sturgis?"

"Oh, I'm fine. I just wanted to thank you for referring us to your cousin."

"How do you know she's my cousin?"

"She told us. She told us all about you. She said you changed your name from Eleanor to Veronica when you were a teenager. She said you're smart but very selfish and that you don't like doing anything for your family that inconveniences you."

I was stunned. Not because my cousin thought I was selfish, I already knew that–we'd had an argument after she kept asking me to chauffeur every geriatric Jew on the West Side of L.A. (and there are legions) to her house for the holidays, and I finally put my foot down. What stunned me was her total breach of ethics. Thanks to her, I now had this lunatic who wasn't even my patient calling me at home to discuss my shortcomings.

"Uh, Sturgis, does your brother know you're calling me?"

"He gave me your number."

"That wasn't very nice of him."

"He's pissed at you because your cousin and her husband spent most of our time arguing with each other about how to do mediation."

"Well, they obviously took a little break from arguing to tell you all about *me*."

"That's true," he said judiciously. Maybe Sturgis was really the *high* functioning brother.

"It's late, Sturgis," I said, because I was damned if I was going to apologize to him for my cousin's bad behavior.

"Well, nice talking to you," he said.

"You bet. Nighty night."

As soon as I hung up, I called my cousin. Her machine picked up.

"Estelle, I got the strangest phone call just now. One of

the two brothers I sent you as a patient referral just called me and he seemed to know my whole life history, which he said you told him. When you get a chance, could you please give me a call? Thanks."

I waited two days for her to get back to me before I called again and left a more assertive message.

"Hey, Estelle, it's your cousin Veronica. You know, *Eleanor*? You must have been having a really bad day when you saw the two brothers I sent you because I heard that you and Len argued with each other during most of the session. I was just trying to do something nice for you, Estelle, in response to your postcard about therapeutic mediation and I think you really fucked me over. How about calling me back and explaining why."

She did not call back. The next day I saw Wilmot, who was twenty minutes late as usual. His arrival was boisterous and disruptive, as if he were being pursued by wolves. He moved like a snowplow through my office, his black hair thick and tousled, his intense, dark eyes bloodshot. He was wearing the same black wool suit he wore to every session, which made him look like a dissolute Hasidic rabbi. And he was bundled up for an arctic expedition, his neck wrapped in a heavy knit yellow scarf, with a marled wool vest covering most of his dingy white dress shirt. He also wore fur-lined leather gloves, heavy black shoes that could have weathered a Minnesota blizzard, and one of those leather pilot hats with earflaps like the squirrel wears in *Rocky and Bullwinkle*. He was constantly worried about "catching a chill," like some old lady, probably his mother, even though it was March and temperatures in Los Angeles rarely dipped below seventy.

"Your cousin's crazy," he said, beginning to disrobe.

"I heard. Look, I'm sorry," I said.

"Boy, does she have a hard-on about you," he said, obviously enjoying this opportunity to torment me.

"Yes, I know. I'm really sorry."

"She wouldn't let her husband get a word in edgewise. I felt kind of sorry for him," he said, stretching himself out on the couch like a sunbathing walrus, his elbows out and palms resting beneath his enormous head.

"Do I sometimes make you feel like you can't get a word in edgewise with *me*, Wilmot?" I asked slyly. Goddammit, I was going to get some psychoanalytic interpretation going; I wasn't about to let the whole patient-analyst relationship disappear down the drain because of my boundary-violating cousin.

"Are you worried that you're like your cousin?" he asked just as slyly, hurling the transference interpretation back at me.

I was definitely feeling off balance, and Wilmot was reveling in my discomfort. He hated his mother, to whom he was pathologically attached, and I was experiencing the rough edge of his maternal rage dragged across my face like a handful of gravel. Just more transference, of course, but he had no intention of letting me interpret that for him. He just wanted me to feel the burn.

And that's how the rest of the session went, me thrusting, him parrying, like Daffy Duck fencing with The Incredible Hulk.

"Don't forget to bring my pink scarf back," I said as he was leaving, all bundled up again as if his next stop was Nome. He had borrowed the scarf back in January when he realized that he'd mistakenly left his at home.

That night I left another message for my cousin. "You've probably cost me my patient, Estelle, so thanks a bunch. What kind of psychologist are you to air your grievances against me with your (or should I say *my*) patient? I think you should surrender your license, Frau Doktor. You're acting as crazy as your crazy father."

Estelle's crazy father Lance (speaking of name changes, his birth name was Larzer) was a handsome, wild-eyed Russian engineer who was fired from every job he ever held and ended up marrying a rich widow who supported his mania and tolerated his chronic unemployment. And *his* mother was even crazier–Lena, a diabetic who, at the age of 88, against all medical advice, insisted for the sake of vanity on having her bunions removed and ended up a double amputee because her poor circulation had caused gangrene.

So it shouldn't really have been a surprise to me that Estelle turned out to be a wacko, but it surprised the hell out of me anyway.

The day before Wilmot's next scheduled appointment, he left me a message saying the usual things patients say when they quit. *Thanks for all your help, I'm feeling pretty good right now, I think I'll take a little break from therapy, ya-da-yada-yada.*

I called him back and left a message of my own. *You owe me for the last two sessions, Wilmot, and I need you to return the pink scarf you borrowed in January.*

Later that afternoon, I received a letter from my cousin. It said, "Dear Eleanor, I am not at liberty to disclose anything that goes on in a patient's session, as you perfectly well know. It's private."

I thought the top of my head would blow off, leaving only my ears and eyebrows. *It's private!* What about *my* privacy? I stormed around my office like a madwoman, screaming at her, telling her what an airhead she was with her trips to Thailand and Turkey and China and all she could say about them was "very interesting!" I made reference to her cooking, which was inedible now that she had eliminated cholesterol. I said her daughter was the inspiration for Miss Piggy and her son had less charm than a moon rock. I told her that her friends were the most boring people I'd ever spent a meal with. I accused her of being jealous and competitive and a manipulative bitch who was always assigning tasks to people, as if we all worked for her, *here, peel the potatoes for the latkes, go pick up Aunt Minnie who pees on the upholstery, and drive my father home*—her demented father Lance who sang the same two lines of "Sunrise Sunset" from *Fiddler on the Roof* until I was ready to throw open the passenger door of my car and push him out onto the freeway.

I said every evil thing I'd ever thought about Estelle, but it didn't dissipate my rage. And then I remembered that she and her husband Jeremy had come all the way up to Santa Barbara for my graduation from therapy school and paid for everyone who joined us for dinner, which must have cost them half a grand. What an ingrate I was, on top of being selfish. I seriously considered returning to analysis.

A few days later, I was finishing up with a delightful new patient a colleague had sent me when the signal light came on from the waiting room - startling me, since no one was scheduled for the next hour. As I led the new patient out, I noticed there was a McDonald's bag with a large grease stain on the end table next to the love seat. Inside was a thank you note from Wilmot with a check for the last two sessions, some Halloween candy–mostly miniature Snickers Bars, and a scarf. It was not *my* scarf, however, which was bulky and rose-colored acrylic that a patient had crocheted for me last Christmas, but rather a cream-colored Ralph Lauren wool scarf with a delicate half-inch of fringe on both ends and the word "cashmere" on the label. I looked it over with frustration, even sniffing it, for fear it would smell like Wilmot, but it only had the greased beef scent of a Big Mac.

Okay, I thought, trying to reason with myself. You lost a patient, but now you have a new one who seems much better suited to analysis and who's willing to pay your full fee. And you got the money for the last two sessions from Wilmot and a better scarf, much better really, than the one you lent him. So?

But I was still fretting, still not satisfied, still full of complaint, because–you know the punchline.

ELAVIL

I was in between Parts I and II of a doomed relationship, living in a body which didn't belong to me, like a slug in someone else's shell. I seemed to be spending all my time in a reclined position, a dissolute Roman after a banquet, glutted and soused on roasted meats and various incarnations of alcohol.

I think I was working on a screenplay with my rich New York writing partner Thomas, who was stashed at the Chateau Belushi, as we referred to the Marmont after John died there, but along with everything else my memory was impaired so I might be conflating two different occasions.

Let's just go with the strong possibility that I was working on a screenplay, it might have been *Families*–about a young couple who kidnaps some abused children from a commune in the '60s–my personal favorite of all the ones we wrote together during our seventeen years as a team, although it never sold ("too European," the agents said, which either meant it didn't follow Syd Field's three-act formula, or it appealed to an audience that occasionally read books).

"I can't get over Rob," I told Thomas, yawning from too much lunch and too little inspiration. Rob was the head of a television production company, a thrice-married man fourteen years older than I was, with several adult children.

"Why don't you write him a letter," Thomas said. And that night I did.

"Dear Rob: Since we're no longer an item, how about giving me a job? I make jokes, I make drinks, I make very little money, so how can you resist? Hugs but no kisses (promise!), Susanna."

Fill in the next fourteen years with whatever you know about doomed relationships. As Tolstoy said, all unhappy relationships are alike. (Okay, that's not what he said, but it's still true.) Nowadays I just check the internet every so often to see if he's dead yet (Rob, not Tolstoy).

Susanna seeks closure, you see.

Actually, Susanna seeks some action. A few more years in the upright position and my vagina will seal over like Chernobyl. And I shall only speak in the third person.

A few more years after that, all my speaking will be confined to séances.

Oh, shut up, Susanna. You're becoming a bore. Go

back on Elavil.

Let me tell you about Elavil, the wonder drug of the seventies with a tiny little side effect that turned every partaker into a jovial Green Bay Packer. In between Parts I and II of my doomed relationship with Rob, I was on Elavil.

It wasn't the first time I had been depressed in my life (nor the last, alas). Every time I lost a relationship, starting with my parents' divorce when I was eight, I got depressed. I don't mean upset, or a little blue, or out of sorts for a couple of weeks, I mean black hole, darkness without end, might-as-well-be-dead-and-rotting-in-a-culvert depressed. But this was the first time that on-the-way-to-becoming-Big Pharma had come up with a drug that could fix it. Yes, there was also Tofranil, but Tofranil just made depressives wander around like serial killer zombies. Elavil, on the other hand, was a magic balloon ride, zippity-do-dah, hi-ho Silver!, thank you, Jesus, and awaaaaay we go!

I'm talking euphoria, sonny boy.

I had been feeling like I was wearing a lead apron I couldn't shed, you know, those ugly gray 'blankets' that med techs drape over you before they zap you with rays. So I asked whichever doctor was in charge of my mental instability at the time for Elavil, having witnessed the miracle it had performed on my previous ex-boyfriend Gabe. Four months after Gabe went on the drug, he became an Elavil spokesperson, talking it up like Marlo Thomas extolling the virtues of St. Jude's.

Four months after that, he left me for a dimple-chinned teenager named Melody.

That was the thing about Elavil, it got your engine going and then there was no stopping you. I went on Elavil just before writing the letter to Rob, so by the time he called me a month later, I was happier than Bugs Bunny in a bowl of carrot salad.

Okay.

Okay, okay, okay.

This is *not* the story of Rob, this is the story of drugs I have known and loved. Elavil was the big one, the one that popped me up like a cork bobbing in the middle of the Pacific Ocean. There was also Oxycodone (I had a legitimate prescription!) and Suboxone, which got me off the Oxy.

But–

I'm not fooling you, am I? You know this isn't a story about drugs, this is a story about men, the men I've loved, and lost, and about being lost after losing them, even though I'm not a loser, not in the other parts of my life, I'm an overachiever in pretty much everything except relationships.

Boo-hoody-hoo.

So here I am, older than I care to admit, and alone, unless you count the eleven pets. Want to know the masterful way I've gone about addressing the problem? I have developed an interest in my ex-husband Axel's best friend,

Nicholas. Nick is a playwright, a director, a fiction writer, and a substitute high school English teacher, but he has not been successful in any of these endeavors. Nick's father was a celebrated Hollywood film editor and Nick was best friends (and shared a girlfriend) with Sam Shepard. Even my ex-husband Axel, his good buddy since high school, was one of the original American Film Institute wunderkinds, but Nick has remained on the sidelines of success, living like a college dropout or a hippy artist in one-room hovels—bitter, sardonic and lecherous. However. In comparison to Axel, who kicked over our TV set (which exploded like a firework) because he was watching too much television, and who stabbed a cheddar cheese to death with a butcher knife in disgust after eating half a wheel, Nick is an angel.

When I was in my early twenties, Nick practically lived with us. Now I only see him once a year, at Thanksgiving, where he makes fun of me and hits on my thirty-year-old goddaughter, Esmeralda, who he says looks just like I did way back when I used to look good.

Hmmmmm.

In other words, he's a perfect choice for Susanna, winner of the Lifetime Achievement Award for Bad Choices.

And he's the only man other than George Clooney who has interested me since Rob.

I was driving him home from Thanksgiving two years ago and he asked me to stop off at Ralph's and pick up some on-sale broccoli and cauliflower. I bought three of each and when he saw the bag, he said, "What the fuck am I going to do with all this?"

"Invite me over?" I asked hopefully.

"Yeah, right," he said with a smirk.

I know that doesn't sound very promising, but this year we have advanced to an exciting new plateau. We are exchanging short stories via email. You know, I'll show you mine if you'll show me yours.

I sent him a nasty little 10-pager about a guy who fucks everybody over but insists he's a victim, from the collection of short stories I'm writing entitled *Was I Wrong to Love You?* Two weeks later, he wrote me a one-word response:

"Cute."

His 25-page story "Seven" (actually 50 pages if it had been properly double spaced) was about a man who wants to fuck seven beautiful women at the same time. Actually, it could have been the same guy that was in my story, now that I think about it.

I wrote Nick a mostly positive critique. Picaresque like J.P. Donleavy's *The Ginger Man.* Good idea to interrupt the consummation of the orgy with several crises, the ex-wife, the runaway teenage daughter, an automobile accident. Lots of misspellings (dinner for diner, instance for instant). Need to double space. Didn't like the part about him having sex with his teenage daughter. Yada yada yada.

At the end of the email, I said, "Should I send another story?" He didn't write back.

I'll see Nick again at Thanksgiving next year if his colon cancer doesn't recur and maybe then he'll realize what a smart, funny, well-preserved woman I truly am.

Or not.

In the meantime, there's a six foot seven inch Jamaican schizophrenic named Julian who I have my eye on. We smile, sweetly and shyly, at each other during our weekly Alanon meetings. (He's in an enmeshed relationship with his mother; I'm in an enmeshed relationship with myself.) My idea is to lure him to my house for dinner and never permit him to leave. Worst case, I'll have to let him bring his mother along, but I've heard (in his deep, soft, lilting Jamaican voice) that she makes a killer curried goat.

A Lion Only Springs Once

After an unusually restless night, Emmy Ann Trehan awoke before dawn with a jolt of clarity and reached over to her husband, taking hold of his shoulder and shaking him.

"Roscoe?" Her voice was high pitched and still a little girlish although she was sixty-eight and as roly-poly as a force-fed goose. "Roscoe, honey?"

Her husband turned toward her and opened his eyes, which were milky blue and blank as a toddler's. He had a short torso, runty legs and more wrinkles than a Shar Pei dog. And his teeth, a few haphazard survivors of drunken accidents and long forgotten fisticuffs, looked more like swine tusks in his loose, deflated mouth.

"We gotta get 'em killed," she said, her voice no different than if she'd told him to pick up a six-pack at the Winn-Dixie. "If there ain't no witnesses, there ain't no trial."

Over a breakfast of Jimmy Dean patties and hotcakes, Emmy Ann laid out the plan, fanning herself with a paper plate as the August morning worked itself up into a scorcher.

"We hafta find someone to do the job," she said, "soon as we come up with five or six hunderd dollars."

"How we gonna do that?" Roscoe asked, pouring more Karo on the sausage because the pancakes had sopped up the first dousing.

"We gotta sell the truck," she said, patting the sweat mustache that glistened above her lip with a damp dishrag.

"Aww, Emmy–" Roscoe protested, half wheeze, half whine. He loved his '88 Ram Pickup like a prize hound.

"We got no choice," she said, her mouth set firm as a block of concrete, and Roscoe knew, as sure as pigs are pork, that his truck was a goner.

Emmy Ann and Roscoe's son Bullard Trehan, a new resident at Elmira's palm-shaded Police Headquarters, looked around suspiciously at the little khaki-colored room that Deputy Nathal Thompson had led him into. He noticed that there wasn't one of those trick mirrors that the laws could look and listen through, only a small, high-up window to the outdoors with bars on it. Not that bars were needed, he thought, with his ankles chained together. He wasn't exactly free to go line dancing at The Buzzard's Lair.

"Sit down, Bullard," Deputy Nathal said, pointing to one of the chairs set up around a bare wooden table. Two half-moons of sweat had already compromised the shirt Nathal's wife had ironed for him that morning, despite the steady wump-wump-wump of the room's ceiling fan. Nathal squinted his eyes and studied Bullard, who he'd known since the third grade, as if his school chum was a familiar farm animal that had suddenly reared up on its hind legs and ordered a Land Shark Lager.

"You gonna grill me again, Nathal?" Bullard asked irritably. "I told you everything already so you ain't gonna get nothing new outta me."

"Your ma and pop are here," Nathal said, offended by Bullard's tone. "They come to visit you."

A minute later, Nathal led Emmy Ann and Roscoe Trehan into the room, pulling out a chair for the old lady and waiting for the dad to settle across from his son before he left them alone.

"Hello, honey," Emmy Ann said, reaching sideways with a loose-skinned arm to give Bullard a hug. "We're gonna fix things for you with the family, honey," she added in a lowered voice. "Don't you worry none."

Bullard looked around uneasily. He hadn't spotted the tiny microphone hidden midway beneath the table, but he'd watched enough TV crime shows in his thirty-one years to smell a rat no matter how much deodorizer it was doused in.

"We oughtn't to be talking here, mama," he said, squirming around in his chair, his soft belly straining against the buttons of his sweaty denim work shirt.

"We sold the truck to Henderson's," Roscoe said, sucking on his lower lip. "Got five hunderd for it."

"All's we need now is to find us a -- whatchamacallit." Emmy Ann paused, searching for a covert way to say it.

"A hit person," Roscoe said in a hoarse whisper.

"I don't think we oughtta–"

"Mum's the word," Emmy Ann said, giving Roscoe the evil eye. "Pop brought you a coupla packs of Camels, sweetheart."

"Nathal took them," Roscoe said, aggrieved. "But he promised to give'em to you later. Can he be trusted?"

"I don't trust no laws," Bullard said.

"Ain't that the truth," his father said, nodding in cahoots.

A few rooms away, Sheriff Ozer clicked off the tape recorder and turned to his deputy.

"I got me a plan, Nathal," he said, winking. "I got me a humdinger of a plan," he said, sounding as gleeful as a bandit in a rich woman's boudoir.

Bullard Trevon had been arrested a month earlier for sexual battery of a child and "lewd and lascivious" molestation. He had allegedly held a gun to his thirteen-year-old stepdaughter's head as he raped her and then threatened to strangle her if she told. But she had told nonetheless, everyone, including her mother, Bullard's wife Nadine, and her six-year-old twin brothers. She also told Sheriff Ozer and his deputy Nathal Thompkins, who'd had a few not-so-holy ideas of his own about his buxom fifteen year-old stepdaughter Rory, truth be told, but he would have never had the nerve to actually lay a hand on her.

Bullard denied that he'd molested his stepdaughter and said she was "a crazy, lying bitch." But the rape kit proved that his DNA was inside her. And that, together with the testimony of his wife, stepdaughter and the twins was more than enough in a good Christian town like Elmira to roast his goose.

The Trehans had at first been troubled by the accusations against their son, the surviving twin they cherished and indulged after losing the other boy to leukemia when he was eight. But when Bullard confided that his wife Nadine had "refused to put out" for over a year, they felt that maybe his behavior was justified. "He just wanted to keep it in the family," Emmy Ann explained to Pastor Roberts at the First Assembly of God Church. "And it t'warant his actual daughter anyways."

But Pastor Roberts was not persuaded. "You've always

let that boy get away with murder, Emmy Ann, and now he's getting his comeuppance."

The pastor offered to pray for Bullard's soul, but Emmy Ann, desperate to keep her son out of jail, wasn't going to depend on heaven to provide a solution.

As the trial grew closer, Elmira's hometown pride took a terrible drubbing. The small, sun-bleached mining town perched on the left shoulder of the Everglades, with a per capita annual income of $16,159, was portrayed by the national news coverage as a stereotypical haven for rednecks who married their pre-adolescent cousins and had sexual relations with the livestock. And when a video of Bullard's arrest went viral on Youtube after he threatened to eat Sheriff Ozer's police dog, Elmira and everyone in it became a national laughingstock. As Carl Hiaasen wrote in his blog about the story, "Sometimes it's not easy to admit that you live in Florida."

But even though Elmira was a humble southern town whose children only received dimes and quarters from the Tooth Fairy, $500 was not enough of an incentive to attract a hit man. So Emmy Ann and Roscoe widened their search, which yielded Hubbard and Hutton, two teenage brothers from the nearby town of Mulberry, who were so enamored of the violent video games in the local arcade that they volunteered to do the job for free. But while Roscoe wanted to take the brothers up on their offer, hoping he could use the money they saved to repurchase his truck from Henderson's Automotive, Emmy Ann put her foot down.

"A lion only springs once, Roscoe," she said, which she had learned from watching the hunting habits of the big cats on Animal Planet. "Those boys would get themselves worked up crazy on marijuana and screw up the plan, maybe just wounding Nadine and the kids, or shooting each other by accident. And how long d'ye think it'd take them to break down and say, "It was all Emmy Ann and Roscoe's idea?"

It was moments like these that reminded Roscoe why he loved his wife so much. Hadn't he said it time and again that it was nothing short of a miracle when she agreed to marry a dumb cluck like him on the luckiest day of his life?

"You're right, honey," he said, and started to weep, grateful that she'd saved him once again from sticking his foot in his ear.

Finally, a friend of a friend of Bullard's cellmate made contact with the Trehans. They were at The Buzzard's Lair enjoying the music and one of the local lagers, as they did every Saturday night except for the month Emmy Ann had her cancer of the uterus surgery, when he sidled up to them.

"Bullard sent me," he said without looking at them, humming something tuneless under his breath. He was a tall, trim fifty-something-year-old with short cropped hair and a sun-weathered face, wearing clean levis and well-worn Frye boots.

"We only got five hunderd," Roscoe blurted out before Emmy Ann could stop him.

"Not here, dumbo," she said with a hiss.

"I'm staying at the Best Western on Mullins Avenue. Call there tomorrow and ask for Ellis Jenkins," he said, and wandered down to the other end of the bar where he ordered a bourbon rocks.

"Well, here we go," Emmy Ann whispered to her husband, her eyes a little wild. She took a long swallow of her lager, hoping to loosen the tightness in her chest.

That night, Emmy Ann appeared to be wrestling with demons, mumbling, cursing and kicking in her sleep, and nearly knocked out one of Roscoe's few remaining teeth when she accidentally fisted him in the mouth.

Roscoe shook her awake, his lip bleeding from the blow. "Emmy Ann, Emmy –?"

"What?!" she said, looking fierce enough to make him draw back from her and cower. Then, feeling a little dazed, she said, "What happened to your lip?"

"You punched me," he said, touching the wound with his tongue.

"I was having a terrible dream, Roscoe," Emmy Ann said. "God was in it, he looked like my father, remember that time when daddy grew the beard and wouldn't shave it off? We had broke Bullard out of jail and we was racing away from the laws in your truck, which I was driving, and God was trying to take the wheel and steer the truck into a ditch. I must've punched you when I was fighting him off, and then we hit a mother deer and her fawn and there was blood all over the windshield and you started screaming like a banshee. . ."

"I better go rinse off my lip," Roscoe said, getting out of bed and stumbling toward the bathroom.

"Maybe we shouldn't go through with it," she said, too softly for him to hear.

"What?"

"I'm sorry, hon," Emmy Ann called out. "Use cold water so it won't swoll up."

The next day, near three in the afternoon, the Trehans arrived at the Best Western and parked Emmy Ann's pea green Honda Civic outside Room 114.

"Let me do the talking, Roscoe," Emmy Ann said as they got out of the car.

"I ain't going to say a word," Roscoe said, clearing his throat and spitting, some of which got caught on one of his teeth and dribbled down past his bruised mouth to his chin.

Inside, the room seemed dark to their eyes after the bright sunlight and for a moment they couldn't spot Ellis

Jenkins, who was sitting on the other side of the bed at the little desk next to the bathroom.

"Did you bring me a key?" he asked.

"We brung you the money and a map of the house," Roscoe said. Emmy Ann glared at him.

"*She'll* tell you," he said, hanging his head.

Emmy Ann fished in her pocketbook for a piece of notebook paper and handed it to Ellis. He studied it for a minute.

"Now who'll be where?" he asked.

Emmy Ann bent over and pointed to a large square in the corner of the map. "This here's where Nadine sleeps," she said. "That's the master bedroom."

"Who's Nadine?"

"Bullard's wife, and let me tell you, she's no prize."

Jenkins grunted noncommittally.

"And this here down the hallway is the twins' bedroom. Right here, see? I put two beds in the drawing, for Clifford and Otis, they're the six-year-olds. And way over here off the kitchen is where Liota sleeps, she's the teenager."

"Three kids and the wife? Who else is there?"

"Just the dog," Roscoe said from the other side of the room."

"You want me to kill the dog?" Jenkins asked.

"Might as well," Emmy Ann said, "if it ain't extra."

"So let me get this straight," Jenkins reiterated. "You want me to kill your daughter-in-law, Nadine, right? And the twins, and the teenage girl?"

"And the dog," Roscoe said. "Garth."

At this point, Sheriff Ozer and Deputy Nathal Thompkins burst through the bathroom door. Emmy Ann began to scream, "Oh, Lord, Lord, Lord, I didn't mean it! God forgive me!" and Roscoe raised his hands up in the air although nobody had asked him to.

It was all on the videotape that was featured on news shows from San Diego to Poughkeepsie as well as on *Nancy Grace*, *Dr. Drew*, *Dr. Phil*, and *YouTube*. It had been a harebrained scheme, of course. How could the Trehans have possibly thought they could get away with it, everyone asked. And didn't they realize that their son could be tried on the basis of the DNA evidence even if there were no witnesses? But no matter how much everybody talked about it, nobody could answer the big question. *How could a pair of grandparents, two church-going Christians at that, decide to commit such a heinous act?*

"Twarn't never about hate," Emmy Ann said when the prosecutor called her heartless during the cross examination. "We was just trying to save our son."

"But they were your grandchildren, your own flesh and blood," the prosecutor persisted.

"We couldn't let ourselves think about that. We had

to blank that out," she said. "God told me it was wrong, but I didn't listen." Then she added, almost hopefully, "It could've been the Devil that took us over. The Devil sometimes does that to Christians, you know."

The Trehans were convicted of attempted murder and conspiracy to commit murder, although the defense claimed entrapment by the undercover lawman Ellis Jenkins.

From behind bars, Emmy Ann ordered Christmas gifts for the kids from Toys 'R Us On Line and had them sent with a card that read, "From your gram and grampa Trehan who love you very much." The daughter-in-law Nadine, who by then was in the process of divorcing Bullard, announced that she and the children were going to make a gigantic holiday bonfire and burn up every single present without even opening them.

Reporters covered the fire for the Christmas Eve news broadcast, which showed a clip of them dancing around the blaze like zombies until something plastic exploded and everybody screamed. And right there with the rest of them, running around barking and snapping at sparks, was Garth the dog, acting like he knew better than any of them about the mysteries of the human heart, and the every-so-often miracle of the good Lord's mercy.

Death Car Girl

There's been a lot of criticism of this woman Ruth Kligman, Jackson Pollock's mistress, mostly by his ugly, jealous wife Lee Krasner. I guess it's because Kligman had let it be known that she wanted to hook up with a great artist and went to the place where he hung out, the Cedar Bar in Manhattan, and snagged him even though she knew he was married. I don't think there was anything wrong with wanting to love a great artist, I might have done the same thing if I knew where to look for one. But I can see Lee Krasner's side, too: she did more than her share of support and put up with Pollock's drunkenness and bad temper and then after he became famous, she got kicked to the curb. I just resent it when the wives blame the mistresses because it's the husbands they ought to be pissed at.

But I wasn't even a mistress this time, although his wife thought I was. His name was Henry, he was a math and science teacher at St. Ignatius Catholic High School in Oakland, California and he was smarter than any three smart people I'd ever known. A big, hunky fellow with a big white sheet cake of a face, big blinky eyes, big horn rim glasses which made his eyes look even bigger, a big snouty nose, big jug handle ears. And homely as a baboon's ass, to be honest, except when he smiled. Then he looked all twinkly with dimples and a devilish glint. And he was really funny in a dry, clever kind of way. Like when he told me that one of his student evaluations had said he was "intelligent but witty." He made me laugh a lot which made me like him a lot but I could never get that to be a sexual attraction, you know what I mean? That's about chemistry and either it's there or it's not.

But it really was there for Henry with me. One time I was coming down the stairs of the little townhouse I was renting in El Cerrito and he just grabbed me and knocked me over and fell on top of me.

"Jesus Christ!" I said and he said "Sorry." He wasn't exactly a smooth operator and that turned me off, too. But I really liked him and I wanted him to stick around so I guess I flirted with him just enough to keep him interested.

He was married to a nursery school teacher named Betsy who he knew since kindergarten back in Macon, Georgia. She was kind of plain and homely like he was with pale white skin that matched her pale blond hair and she was pregnant and he was so depressed that he kept thinking he was going to have to kill himself because he didn't love her anymore but he couldn't bring himself to leave her.

"The one time I tried to get away, I crashed my Harley into a Burger King. Took out the entire salad bar and broke three ribs," he said. "But it's not Betsy's fault, she's a wonderful person."

I didn't know what to tell him. Damned if he did or didn't, I thought.

"Let's you and me run away together, Red," he said. He called me Red because of my hair, even though my name was Sally.

"Not today," I said, trying to keep it light. "I have to wash the dog." (I didn't have a dog.)

"It's about time," Henry drawled. "That dog was beginning to stink up the place."

Henry told me all kinds of fascinating, poetic things about science like Heisenberg's Theory of Electron Probability and the double helix and the blackness of black holes. He said that before The Big Bang there was absolute chaos, which was synonymous with nothingness.

"Now get this. The Hebrew word in the Bible that describes the universe before Creation means *chaos and nothingness*. They're synonymous!"

"Wow," I said. "Wow, wow, wow."

"See, the reason religious people can't reconcile science with faith," he said, "is because they don't believe that God, who created the whole universe, can create metaphor!"

I really wished that I could fall in love with Henry because he had a very sexy brain. But the rest of him was like a big ugly mud hut with a dead grass roof and I just couldn't get past that. Not that I was Angelina Jolie or anything, but at least I was cute.

I had met Henry drinking coffee and eating banana cream pie in the lunch room at St. Ignatius. I was an intern there getting my hours of teaching experience so I could get a credential in high school English. Teaching wasn't what I really wanted to do, I wanted to be a great poet, but even great poets have to work for a living, at least in America they do. Like Wallace Stevens: he was vice president of an insurance company, and William Carlos Williams was a doctor.

Anyway, things got all messed up between me and Henry the night my mother died. I was really upset and crying my eyes out, even though I had known for a long time that she had terminal cancer and was going to die. When Henry found out, he came over and made dinner for me, macaroni and cheese and broccoli, and he was really sweet and even brought me a wet washrag to clean off my face which was covered with tears and snot and he even cleaned it off for me like I was a little helpless girl.

So I thought I should do something nice to thank him, just a little BJ in the living room, I didn't even kiss him or anything. But he got all crazy after that and went home and told his wife that we were in love with each other.

"What the fuck, Henry," I said when he told me, "what the fuck!"

Next thing, his wife found out where I lived and came over. She was so pregnant I thought she was going to have the baby right in front of me, and she called me a tramp and then she started to cry and begged me not to take Henry away from her.

"Listen, Betsy," I said, "swear to God, I don't want to take Henry away from you. We're just friends and I don't know why he told you that stupid thing about us being in love with each other but it isn't true!"

I made her some peppermint herbal tea and she told me the story of her life, how she was the youngest of three sisters in Macon and how her father had to raise them the best he could after their mother died and how Henry and she met in the first grade and how he proposed to her in the second grade and every year after that until they were in college and how scared she was about being a mother for the first time and even more scared that Henry would leave her alone with the baby so far away from her sisters back in Georgia and what was she supposed to do?

I felt pretty bad for her and told her I'd babysit for her if she ever needed help. She gave me a big hug when she left and said she was glad we were friends now, and I said yes, and said everything was going to be okay.

After that, I stayed as far away from Henry as possible and only heard through the grapevine that he and Betsy had had a little boy.

It was about six months later that Henry came by my

townhouse. He just showed up without calling first. When I opened the door he was standing there kind of sheepish with his little boy in one of those slings so of course I asked him to come inside.

He was really proud of the little fellow, Marcus he said was the name. I tried to think of something nice to say about the baby but I'll tell you, that thing about how all babies are beautiful is bullshit because Marcus looked exactly like Henry. His nose was so big that I wondered if the rest of his face would ever catch up.

"He's really big," I said finally and that seemed to please Henry.

"He looks just like my brothers," Henry said, "It's amazing." I pictured a whole family of big, homely kids in Macon, Georgia with big noses and horn rim glasses and two homely parents and an ugly dog.

"You look really happy," I said.

"I am," he said and I felt relieved for Betsy.

But around Thanksgiving I heard from one of the other St. Ignatius interns that Henry was having an affair with the social studies and health teacher Lillian Birdsong, kind of a skinny gal with an overbite and that wispy brown hair that looks fried. And the day after Thanksgiving, Black Friday, it was all over the news. "High school teacher killed in five car pile-up on the I-80."

It was poor Lillian Birdsong who had got killed. Henry had only sustained head injuries, a collapsed lung and broken legs. They were running off together to Reno, the newscasters said. "Let's you and me run away together, Lillian," he had probably said. And she, the poor dummy, had said yes.

All that weekend I kept seeing pictures of Henry's Toyota on the TV and in the newspaper. It didn't look like a Toyota anymore, it looked like one of those Rauschenberg recycled junk sculptures, with its twisted grill snarling like some old Edward G. Robinson gangster and two raggedy, empty eye sockets where the headlights had been. If it could have talked, it probably would have said, "What the fuck, Henry."

I heard later that Henry went back to his wife when he got out of the hospital and after the first of the year, they both moved back to Macon. I figured his guilt had a lot to do with the accident. When all was said and done, Henry was a very moral man.

I felt pretty lucky about not falling in love with Henry because if I had it would have been me all crashed up and dead in that car accident. I was like Ruth Kligman, who everyone called the "death car girl" because she had lived through the car crash that killed Jackson Pollock and her girlfriend Edith Metzger. Ruth Kligman was a survivor. One year after Pollock died, she shacked up with another great artist who was much better looking, Willem de Kooning.

But she was luckier than I am, I haven't met any great

artists, handsome or otherwise, or even another brilliant homely guy like Henry. I did fall in love with a married poetry teacher at UC Berkeley during spring quarter, but when I realized I had just confused him with William Carlos Williams because he wrote a book about Patterson, it was all over for me. The closest I ever came to greatness was Billy Collins. I sent him one of my poems when I was 16 and he sent me a postcard from Florida that said, "Good poem, kiddo. Keep writing."

Lately I've been writing a lot of poetry, some of it's about my crazy family of lapsed and "recovering" Catholics but also about Henry, Lillian Birdsong and my survivor's guilt from the accident because I keep feeling like it's kind of my fault that she died. I write about the things Henry told me, too, like the double helix and black holes, which by the way I think are two of God's truly great metaphors. Some guy told me recently that the stuff Henry said about the universe was junk physics and crap, and I thought maybe that was my fault because I wasn't saying it right, but to tell you the truth, that guy was trying to get in my pants and I think he just wanted to prove he was smarter than Henry when he really wasn't.

I've just about given up on men, especially married ones, at least for the time being until I get my head on straight. I've even begun to wonder sometimes if maybe the great artist I keep looking for might have to be me.

OMG, as my students say. It's pretty daunting.

HOBGOBLINS

It is November 1. When I went to sleep three hours ago, it was still Halloween, although the doorbell had finally stopped chiming, the miniature Mounds and Snickers and M&M's with Peanuts had run out, and Batman and Spider-man and Superman and Princess Fiona had finally retired to Fantasyland for another 364 days.

It is 3 a.m. and the phone is ringing. Nothing good comes of a phone call at 3 a.m. I sit bolt upright, reaching around for my glasses on the dresser top next to my bed, in the process knocking over the Trazadone bottle, the ibuprofen bottle and the half-empty Diet Coke can which spills all over my nightgown and into my fleecy bedroom slippers.

"Awww, nuts," I say, groping for the phone which has now rung twice. Amelia Bedelia my Doberman, disrupted from sleep by my clumsy acrobatics and the Coke spill, stands up in bed, opens her mouth and yawns with a high pitched squeal that awakens Mitchell my cat, who rolls over on his back too close to the edge of the bed and drops onto the bare wood floor with a thud. My hand is shaking when I finally grasp the phone because I am a mother and 3 a.m. calls trigger my worst nightmares.

"Hello," I say, sounding childlike and half-asleep.

"Mom?" It is whispered.

Fully awake and instantly adult, I say, "What's wrong?"

"I'm with Fritz."

"What's wrong?" I ask louder.

"He's standing in the corner talking to the devil."

"What?"

"He's talking to the devil."

"Are you dressed? Get out of there."

"I don't want to upset him."

"He's already upset, get out of there."

"He's never done this before. I think Halloween got to him."

Edie has been seeing this hair dresser, Fritz, for the last month, his claim to fame that he trims her bangs perfectly. I picture the scissors and have a horrific vision of him trimming her flesh.

"Who cares if he's never done it before? He's doing it now."

"Don't get mad at me."

"I'm not mad at you. I'm scared to death *at you.*"

"Just don't yell."

"I'm not yelling," I say, lowering my voice. "Listen to me. Get dressed. Are you dressed?"

"No."

"Get dressed."

"Can you talk to him?"

Can I talk to him?

Before I can answer *hell no!* she says, "Here," and hands Fritz the phone.

"Hello, Mrs. Waller," he says, sounding like Eddie Haskell in *Leave It To Beaver*. I am not Mrs. Waller, that is the name of the woman Edie's father is currently married to, thank heavens, but I don't correct him.

"Hi, Fritz. How's it going?"

"Not so good."

"Did you take a drug, Fritz? Are you having a bad trip?"

"No."

Oh great, he's having a psychotic break, I think, because I am in my last year of psychotherapy school, my fifth career, and I know a little about psychotic breaks.

"Edie says you're talking to the devil, Fritz."

"Uh-huh."

"What's on the devil's mind?"

"He says I'm a bad person."

"You are not a bad person, Fritz. Don't you know the devil lies his ass off about things like that? Remember how he lied to Eve about the apple and got us all kicked out of Eden? He's lying to you, Fritz."

"Okay."

"You're a very nice person."

"Thank you."

"And Edie says you're a great hair stylist."

"Thank you."

"Tell you what, Fritz, I'll come into your shop tomorrow and you can cut my hair, okay?

"Okay."

"But you know what you should do now? You should tell Edie to go home so you can get a good night's sleep."

"Okay." I hear him tell Edie that she has to go home.

"Mom?" Edie takes the phone back.

"You heard him. Go home."

"Will Fritz be okay?"

For all I know, Fritz will run off and join Cirque du Soleil or climb up on the roof and try to contact Pluto.

"Yes, Fritz will be fine. Did you drive to his house?"

"Uh-huh."

"Good. Drive home," I say, relieved that I will not have to go there and get her, trying to sound calm and sweet, even though I want to scream at the top of my lungs, *"Get the fuck out of there, you lunatic, before he turns you into human hash browns."*

"Okay," she says and hangs up.

"Wait–" I shout, wanting to tell her to call me as soon as she gets home. "Shit shit shit," I say, slamming the phone back in its cradle, which causes it to bounce off and strike me in the forehead. Amelia Bedelia gives me a mournful look and takes off for the tranquility of the sofa in the living room. Mitchell has already gone out the half-open window into the autumn chill of early morning.

I wait five minutes and call Edie's home phone. Nothing. I begin calling every other minute. By the tenth call, I have already exchanged my pajamas for sweats and am ready to head for Mt. Washington to look for her.

She picks up.

"Hi," she says casually, as if nothing bizarre had just happened.

"Edie," I say. "What is it with you? Why are you a magnet for psychotics?"

"Eliot wasn't psychotic. He was manic depressive."

"That's a psychosis," I say, having received an A+ in my Abnormal Psychology class.

"Oh."

"You can't be with Fritz any more. Do you hear me?"

"Uh-huh. What do I do if he calls?"

"Hang up."

"What if he comes over?"

"Don't let him in." I feel like I'm talking to a child rather than a 26-year-old college graduate who was just voted the top designer clothing saleswoman at Bloomingdale's Century City, and who makes more money than I do.

"I know I've been a very bad example, honey," I say, trying to stick to my family therapy *mea culpa* script. "I've had a lot of crazy boyfriends, starting with your father and I've subjected you to more drama than a daytime soap. But I've learned my lesson, Edie. Can't you learn your lesson, too?"

"Okay," she says, yawning.

"Go to sleep," I say. "Is your door locked?"

"Uh-huh."

"I love you," I say, feeling as if it might have been the last time I got to tell her that.

"Me too," she says, half asleep.

I climb back under the covers and close my eyes. My heart is beating very fast and I doubt if I'll be able to get back to sleep. I listen to the tail end of *Natural Born Killers* on HBO and nod off with Robert Downey Jr.'s voice in my ear.

The devil comes to me in a dream. He says, "Ha ha ha," like we have been playing Hide and Seek and he has just discovered me in the tiny storage closet under the stairs, hidden behind the bicycle pump, the sleeping bags and my dead mother's hat boxes. "Ha ha ha," he says again, looking suspiciously like Edie's father.

"Go away," I say. "Halloween's over."

He narrows his feline yellow eyes, lurches forward on his cloven hooves and says, "Don't you wish."

Bathing Beauty

The whole city was steaming and we were the clams. The insides of my thighs were sticking together like someone'd slopped glue on them, and it wasn't exactly perfume that I smelled coming from under my arms and between my legs.

Time for a bath, I announced to nobody in particular. I went upstairs to run the water, leaving Dick, my current flame and Jackson, my ex, yakking it up about catalytic converters, axle ratios and drag coefficients, which they could have done all night and half of tomorrow probably.

Actually, it tickled me to see those boys getting along so well, especially since one was the father and one was the step. I was more the intellectual, artistic type but I liked men who knew how to build things and fix things. All you had to do was take a look at Sylvia Plath and Ted Hughes to see that no family needed two poets. And it wasn't any better for painters—check out what Diego Rivera did to

Frida Kahlo. Better to make relationships out of mongrels was my theory. It hadn't worked so far, but–well, it had worked for a while and then it hadn't. But Dick was a sweetheart, and BJ liked him.

"Can someone bring me up a Diet Coke?" I yelled from the tub.

A few minutes later, up comes Dick with an ice cold can. Before I can pop the top, Jackson walks in. They're still talking car shit, something about airfoils.

"It corners like Road Runner, but how do you live with the drag?" Dick says.

"Did you guys know there's a very important automobile in *The Great Gatsby*? A green something-or-other, I think it was a Packard."

They looked at me as if I had just farted into the bathwater. Two big guys, tall, heavyset, handsome in different ways, Jackson dark and almost pretty, Dick light and rugged, with one of those Roman noses. And here I was, small and wiry like a capuchin monkey.

I continued. "You know that French Impressionist painting of the naked lady at a picnic with a couple of men in suits?" I said. "*Dejeuner Sur l'Herbe*?"

"What are you talking about?" Jackson said.

"I'm talking about how it's a little weird that I'm sitting in the bathtub naked and you're both in here hanging out like we're having a picnic or something."

"Well," Dick said, sitting down on the toilet seat, "it's not like, you know, uh, we both, uh, well–" He looked over at Jackson for help.

"Been there, done that," Jackson said.

"Yeah," Dick said, "exactly," laughing a little.

"Oh," I said, "so I'm just some old car you've both already driven," I said.

"Yeah," Dick said agreeably, but Jackson was more cautious.

"Not an *old* car," he said. "Just a car."

"Well, I feel much better now," I said, enjoying his discomfort.

"A classic car," Jackson added.

"Runs like a jackrabbit," Dick chimed in, forgetting that they were supposed to be talking about me, thinking about the 1970 Datsun Fairlady Roadster that he had just finished restoring.

Jackson reached into the tub and splashed a little water on my breasts. "Planning to prune?" he said.

Dick stood up and lifted the toilet seat.

"Honey!" I hollered, "pee downstairs, okay?" Somehow, me being naked plus Dick whipping out his wizzer was one too much.

"Okay." Dick shrugged good-naturedly and left. "Goin' out to the garage, Jack," he called after.

"Got it," Jackson called back. He put the toilet seat down and sat.

"So," he said.

"So," I said.

"Seems like a good guy."

"You make a handsome couple," I said.

Jackson grabbed the bath towel off the floor and dropped it on top of me.

"Hey," I said.

"Hey yourself," he said.

I stood up, covered in towel, and stepped out carefully onto the tile.

"Well, Jackson," I said, starting to dry myself off, "this was a moment I never imagined when you and I were hot and heavy." Jackson took the towel from me and patted my shoulders and back.

"Did you ever imagine being thirty?" he said, draping the towel over the shower curtain rack.

"No, I never imagined that either," I said.

"My point."

He opened the medicine cabinet and stared at the shelves of nose drops, Vicks Vaporub, Valerian root and Band-Aids. I pulled a clean white tee shirt over my head and slid into a pair of shorts.

Jackson snapped the cabinet shut, took his index finger

and drew a little heart on the steamy mirror.

I thought to myself that this must be why men liked having harems and wouldn't it be interesting to have two men around.

"So much for imagination," he said, taking a sip of the half-empty mostly fizzed out Coke before he walked off down the hall.

That was the thing about Jackson. He could always read my mind.

GREYHOUNDS

When you don't fly or drive or train, you are relegated to the bus, more accommodating than a boxcar to Auschwitz but perilously close to a sleepover in a homeless shelter. Still, my travels on Greyhounds have afforded me adventures I would otherwise never have experienced, an enforced human intimacy that I, an unmarried executive in my thirties, wouldn't have traded for all the perks and pampering in the world.

All aboard a mud-spattered silver carriage in downtown Phoenix at 11:10 p.m. after a long day of meetings with, among other people, my nemesis, Daniel Frost. The poster boy for corporate sociopathy, always the thin-lipped smile and the unblinking stare of a reptile, waiting for the tiniest lapse in attention to envenomate helpless prey.

"Are you a cripple?" he once asked, referring to my temporary limp from a broken toe. "Cripples give me the creeps."

Another time, he grabbed my face in one of his ham-sized hands and proclaimed, "Even with make-up you're not much to look at, Adele."

Now I could sue him for harassment in the workplace, but back then I just smarted in silence.

On this particular day in Phoenix, however, vengeance was mine. Right after Frost, with the salivating glee of a komodo, spotted the price tag still hanging from the under-arm of my new white linen suit, he was informed that his vice presidency had been put on hold pending the outcome of an allegation that he'd embezzled a quarter million dollars from the company.

However, the highlight of my day didn't occur in the board room, but rather, on the bus ride back to Los Angeles. We, by which I mean me and the other 46 passengers, had been plagued since Tolleson by the rant of a deranged, hoarse-voiced rider, regarding the *shitassed motherfuckers* who fucked up the *shitassed world* and *every fucking asshole* and *bitchcunt* in it, leaving the *shiteaters* even more fucked up than *the motherfucking motherfuckers* could fucking know if they fucking knew anything which *they fucking well* didn't.

When we reached Indio, several of us, including the disgruntled rager, got off the bus, possibly to use a less malodorous toilet, or purchase a dust-encrusted "genuine Indio palm tree replica keychain," or simply to rest our beleaguered eardrums and stretch our miserably cramped legs. But when we reboarded twelve minutes later, our blaspheming nemesis was MIA.

"Everybody back on board?" the driver asked, scrutinizing our exhausted faces in his rearview mirror.

We looked around at each other uncertainly until one brave traveler shouted, "Yes!" Inspired by his example, we formed an instantly harmonious chorus, chanting more yeses than Molly Bloom in the last forty pages of *Ulysses.*

A moment later, amidst celebratory cheers and raucous laughter, as if we were war buddies linked for life by our communal courage, the Greyhound took off into the pale white light of early dawn, moving toward home even faster than the leggy, fog-colored dogs that gave it its name.

Mothership Down

I hear voices, low and high, drinking and laughing but I cannot open my eyes. There is a party going on but I have not been invited. I want to go to the party. Open, open, open, I say to my eyelids but they will not obey. They are oppo–oppi? I cannot remember the words for what they are. There are two words; I can almost see them but I cannot remember them.

Someone is talking to me. She says, "It's time to wake up. Can you wake up?" I open my eyes. She is black but she is all white. Black and white? The bed is moving. Uh-oh. A breeze is floating across my face like butterflies. Whoo-whoo-whoosh. I see light light light light light light, then flash flash flash they are taking my picture, no, wait, my hair is not combed. I wet my lips and try to smile.

Lights out.

Dark now. I want to sit up but my body won't move. Up, I tell it. Nothing. Up. Nothing. I can move my neck. I see other people but I don't know who they are. "Hello?" I say.

There is a sharp slice of light. It is coming from outside the room. Someone walks by.

"Hello," I say. "Help," I say. He stops, looks at me. He is green and black. "Help," I say again.

"Okay," he says. He walks away.

"No, no," I say, "come back."

I feel wet on my face. My tongue snails out, finds salt. Uh-oh, I am crying.

I wake up. The room is too bright. I see people I don't know, they are all around me in jammy tops. I am in a jammy top, too. Pink. Little bears and elephants. A wrinkly old woman next to me has giraffes and monkeys. Yellow. She has no teeth, someone stole her teeth. I open and close my mouth. Click-click. Teeth are still there, they didn't steal my teeth. Who are "they?"

A green man comes in the room. He is rolling something silver that is noisy. It smells greasy like French fries.

"Breakfast," he says. "Who's hungry?"

"I am very hungry," I say.

"Good," he says, and reaches behind me, lifting me up

to sit with two pillows.

"Owww," I say. "Ooooooh."

He takes one pillow away.

"Better?"

"Yes," I say. But I am crying again. He gives me a plastic plate with brown egg and potatoes and something cold and pukey-looking. I stick my finger in it and put the finger in my mouth. Apple sauce, *ugh,* too sweet. I eat a little brown square of potato. *Ummmmm.* What is that called? Little square potatoes? Why can't I remember the–*ummmmmmm.* I am so hungry.

The green man is giving plastic plates to other people. The lady with no teeth is eating apple sauce. Her mouth makes slapping, sucking noises. Someone stole her teeth. I check my mouth again. Teeth still there.

My daughter Isobel is here, but how? I tried to call her before but they have done something to the phone. I don't know who *they* are, but they have messed with the phone. I try and try but cannot make it dial her number. I think Dr. Bromberg does not want me to tell her that I hate the hospital. But here she is anyway.

"I don't like it here," I say. "They tie me to the bed at night."

"They don't want you to get out of bed yet, mom. You were in surgery for ten hours. You're supposed to stay down."

"Ten hours?" I am surprised. "What does Doctor Bromberg say I am? Oppi-something."

"He says you are oppositionally defiant."

"That's right. Oppi-defiant."

"Yes, you certainly are," Isobel says.

"I am peeing now," I say, having the warm feeling I have felt several times, "but where is it going?"

Isobel lifts my blanket and points to a tube that is coming out from the bottom of my jammy top. I see yellow in the tube.

"That's my pee," I say, smiling. I don't know why I am smiling.

"Yes," she says. "That's right." She sounds like Mrs. Dickenson, my nursery school teacher with the wavy white hair when I was three. *That's very good, Jackie*, she used to say when I drank up all my milk.

When Isobel comes to see me again, I am playing poker with one of the green men, young, very thin, with a mustache. I am winning. I never remember the rules but I always win at poker.

"This is Gerald," I say, introducing Isobel to the green man.

"I know Gerald, mom. You introduced me yesterday."

"And the day before," Gerald says.

"Gerald is gay," I say in a loud voice, trying to remember how to arrange my cards.

"Mom! Don't say that."

"No," I say, "it's okay. Gerald needs to accept that he is gay. I'm a therapist, Gerald, so I know these things. I have one-and-a-half Ph.Ds."

"Mom, please," Isobel says, looking around at the other people in the room. Her face is red.

"They know, too," I say, meaning the other people in the room. "It's not a secret, Izzy."

"Not anymore," Gerald says, laying down two cards.
"I'm sorry," Isobel says to Gerald.

"There's nothing to be sorry about," I say, laying down 6-7-8-9-10 hearts. "Can you bring me my business cards, Izz? I want the patients to come see me when they get out of the hospital. Gerald, too."

"You can't do that, mom. You're a patient, too."

"Lots of the people here need help, Izzy. I can help them."

"How about helping yourself first," Gerald says.

I glare at him. I consider biting him.

"You're just jealous because I have one-and-a-half Ph.Ds and you have none, Gerald."

"Mom!" Izzy says.

"It's okay," I whisper loudly. "I'm just trying to get him to go back to school."

It is several days later, or a few, I don't know how many. When they pull the pee-pee tube out, I get up and walk around the big room. Then I sit down. Then I get up again. I sit down. Then I get up again. My back hurts where the doctors cut me. There is no TV. That's how I know it is a shitty hospital. I tell Dr. Bromberg that he has a shitty hospital. He smiles at me like I am not hurting his feelings but I know I am. I can't help it. It is a shitty hospital with no TV.

One day when no green men are around, not even Gerald, I walk around the hospital. There are TVs in some of the rooms with only one or two people. I go into a room and sit down. There is a very old person in the bed, a man or a woman, with lots of tubes sticking out, not just a pee-pee tube. We watch "Let's Make a Deal," but Monty Hall is gone. Where happened to Monty Hall?

Come on down!

I walk around some more. I look into rooms and see sick people with gray faces and wide open mouths with no teeth. I am not sick. I came here to get my back fixed and now it is fixed. I have to get back to work, my patients are waiting for me.

I find a gift store but it is locked. It says, "Be back soon" on the door, so I wait. I wait and wait because I love gift stores. Finally, a lady comes back and opens the door. I go in and look around. There is a big mirror. I look at my face. My hair is down to my shoulders. It looks young, except for the silver hairs mixed in with the brown. But my face is pale and tired. I smile. Now I look like a very old princess. I walk around the store and find many things I want. A tattoo kit with dragons and dinosaurs, a stationary set that has the initial J for Jackie which is my name (actually Jacqueline), a cream-colored tea set from England with little flowers painted on each cup and saucer, and a beautiful red pen so I can write letters and tell everybody what a shitty hospital this is.

I bring them all up to the front where the cash register is. "Just charge these to my room," I say.

"This is not a hotel."

"No? I'll get my purse and come back." I am heading out the door when I see Isobel.

"Mom!" she says, looking upset, "where were you?"

"I was here," I say. I take her hand and lead her to the cash register.

"The hospital called me. They've been looking all over for you," she says.

"I was here," I say again. "Can you pay for these things? I just have to find my pocketbook, but I think somebody stole it."

"I have your pocketbook, Mom. Remember I took it before you went into surgery?"

"Oh, yes," I say, pretending to remember. I don't want her to know that I can't remember anymore, because I used to remember everything, like an elephant.

"You can't just wander around the hospital, Mom," Isobel says, giving the lady at the cash register her credit card.

"Okay," I say, peeking into the bag of new things I have bought.

"I got a new pen," I say, feeling excited about all the letters I can write now. Then I remember that I have been having trouble writing. The words get stuck in my brain and I can't pull them out.

"I think the doctors put glue in my brain when I was asleep, Izzy," I whisper.

"It's the medicine the surgeon gave you, mom. Decadron. It made you a little crazy."

"Oh, is that so?" I ask, trying to remember the name that she has just told me but already forgetting it. "Will it go away?"

"Yes," she says, but she looks worried.

Isobel has read my mind and brought me a sandwich from Whole Foods. It has everything in it. Turkey and corned beef and coleslaw and pickles and tomato and lettuce and mustard and secret sauce like MacDonald's.

As I am eating, I see that Gerald is feeding soup to the

old woman next to my bed with a big silver spoon. She makes loud slurpy sucky gurgling sounds.

I lean over to Isobel and whisper loudly, "They stole her teeth."

"Shhh, mom," she says and her face is red again.

"Mine are still there," I say, opening my mouth wide so she can see. My mouth is full of turkey and rye bread and pickle and tomato.

"Mom," Isobel says, "close your mouth, for God's sake."

I close my mouth but I am laughing so hard that food leaks out and runs down my chin.

"Dr. Bamburg wants you to go to the UCLA hospital, Mom," Isobel says, "so you can get over the Decadron."

"He hates me," I say.

"No, he doesn't. He wants you to get better."

"I *am* all better. I want to go home," I say, my mouth tired of chewing on so much sandwich.

"You can't go home yet," she says.

"Yes I can."

"No."

"Okay, fine!" I say, getting weepy. "I don't know anything," I say, and more food juice leaks out of my mouth.

"Yes you do, Mom, you're the smartest person in the world," she says, trying to wipe my mouth with a napkin.

"No," I say, taking another bite of sandwich. "No, no, no," I say, choking a little, and put the sandwich down on the bed. My hands sit in my lap like two dead fish.

"I used to know everything but not anymore," I say.

"Don't say that, Mommy," Isobel says and starts to cry.

"Okay," I say, and stop crying because I want her to cheer up. "I know something. Want to know what I know?"

"Yes," Isobel says and blows her nose in a Kleenex.

"I know how to sing "A Birdie with a Yellow Bill" in Japanese." My father taught me when I was four.

"Ka-waa-ee-ee-ka-to-oh-ree, ko-ma-do-nee-taw-awn-day, oh-meh-meh-wah-pa-chee-koo-ree, oh-neh-bo-no-neh-bo-chan."

A few people in the room applaud. Gerald says "Bravo!"

"Thank you, thank you," I say, feeling proud because I remembered it perfectly.

Isobel sits down next to me on the bed and takes my hand. Most of the sad is gone from her face and I am relieved. Maybe it's good, I think, that I am so small. Maybe now Isobel can get big.

"You know what else I know, Izzy?"

"What?" she says.

"I'll be back!" For some reason, I say it with a German accent.

Gerald says, "It's the *Governator*!"

"What?" I ask, not comprehending.

"That's what *The Terminator* says, Mom. Arnold Schwarzenegger." Isobel is giggling.

I don't know what's funny but I like to make her laugh.

"I'll be back!" I say again, loud, like a superhero. It reminds me of someone. Me?

"I hope so," she says.

Red Flags

Introduction

You know how women say, "He seemed so perfect. How could I possibly know that he was a raging alcoholic, or a pathological liar, or a compulsive philanderer? The simple answer is that there are *always* red flags.

Always.

As in Captain frigging Obvious.

Exhibit A

They met for the first time after his UC Berkeley guest lecture on Maya Deren's surrealist films. She was flirty and he was horny and they strolled to a café on Telegraph Avenue called *Le Bateau Ivre* (Rimbaud, 19th century French poet, am I underestimating you by telling you this?).

She asked him all about New Haven because she had just been hired to teach Italian literature at Yale, and he was already a professor of Art History at Yale, and he told her he was in the process of divorcing his wife and she told him she was in the process of breaking up with her rock musician boyfriend and he pretended to be so fascinated by every word that came out of her mouth that she mistook him for a good listener.

That was the first red flag.

Exhibit B

After she moved to New Haven, they went to see a revival of Martin Scorsese's *Mean Streets*, and afterward he said that the characters "disgusted" him because they were "so low class."

So, Italians are low class? she said, and he said, *Not all Italians. Not you, Gina.*

That was the second red flag.

<u>Exhibit C</u>

The third red flag, which was not entirely unrelated to the second one, was when her five-year-old daughter Caroline discovered that his wealthy Darien parents didn't sleep in the same bed, or even in the same bedroom, and had the temerity to ask them *why?* Their faces froze and cracked like they'd been dipped in liquid nitrogen and he said, *Car-*

oline, for fuck's sake, you have no manners!

Come to think of it, there were a lot more than three red flags. Like the number of women he had slept with during his eighteen-year marriage: 674. (He counted.) But apparently he did not consider *that* a lack of good manners.

Or the fact that he drank half-gallons of cheap Chablis every single day and both his father and older brother were alcoholics.

Not to mention that his name was Miles Standish (MacGregor) and he referred to himself, proudly, as a Mayflower WASP and tried to hide the fact that his baby sister Celeste was currently living with a 300 pound LGBTQ named Juanita.

Even a fool could have seen that they were totally wrong for each other.

1. He wanted to have sex ten times a day. (Okay, maybe not ten, but at least six or seven.)

She faked orgasms.

He admitted that he didn't really listen to her.

He didn't like Italians.

She began to hate him each time he called and said, "I'm just checking in." She wanted to say, "I'm just checking out."

They kept running out of conversation. One time they

were up in Boston for his lecture on Man Ray and neither of them could come up with anything that involved words. It was like their brains had experienced a simultaneous power surge that totally fried their vocabularies.

Then there was the time he took her ice skating and she was so depressed she couldn't even lace her skates, so she just sat on the bench all catatonic until he lost his temper, laced them up for her and yanked her onto her feet like a rag doll.

There were plenty of warning signs that the romance was wearing off:

A. She stopped faking orgasms.

B. He started checking out other women. He wasn't even all that handsome, but women were just crazy about him. At first when he and Gina went to parties, all the females gave her dirty looks. But after a while they acted like she wasn't even there and he went off into dark corners with them and pretended to listen.

C. When she told him that she'd take care of his daughters if anything ever happened to him, he said, "I really can't promise that I'd take care of Caroline. I mean, we don't even like each other so it wouldn't be fair to either of us."

(Cf. p. 4, item 7 – reason for depression at the ice skating rink)

<u>Gina's Rationalization (There's *always* a rationalization!)</u>

It had been so romantic* at first. He wanted to have sex with her six or seven times a day, like he was on a Viagra drip or something, and he could do amazing things with his tongue. He even wrote her love letters, which no other man had ever done. To be honest, the letters were too long and kind of corny. And she really didn't enjoy having sex so many times a day. But she liked having a man be crazy about her because she was used to it being the other way around.

<u>Sidebar</u>

Merriam-Webster's definition of *romantic*: "Having no basis in fact; imaginary; impractical in conception or plan.

<u>The Backstory</u>

They'd had a big fight after the first time they had sex when he admitted he was still living with his wife (that was another red flag). He also revealed that he had a couple of girlfriends up in Boston and one in San Francisco that he hated having to give up (another *big* red flag), so she told him to go fuck himself and stormed out of his office crying.

But then he spent the whole weekend looking for her, driving all over New Haven until he spotted her silver Pacer in the Italian neighborhood where she'd rented a little house, and finally found her, scrubbing the bathtub when he came through the screen door like a big gust of wind and climbed up the stairs and she thought he was a rapist or a murderer until she saw it was him and they had sex on the bathroom tile right next to the toilet and it was all so bodice-ripping romantic until he had to leave because it was his turn to take his daughters to soccer practice.

Coda

When she waved goodbye from the front porch and saw him smiling at her all lovey-dovey and mushy as a mashed banana inside his big, dirty red van, his face suddenly transformed into a melted Halloween mask of serial murderer John Wayne Gacy, "the Killer Clown."

"Euuu!" as her college roommate Meryl used to say, "don't go soft on me, for fuck's sake." Gina wanted to run as far away as she could get on two legs and never set eyes on him again. (This belongs in the "all wrong for each other" section, or maybe a new section called "Fantasy Spoiler" or "Reality Alert!")

Reversal of Fortune

When he told her at the end of the academic year that he had decided to take a tenured teaching job in the Art History Department at UC Santa Cruz and didn't want her to come with him, she went completely berserk like there hadn't been any red flags or warning signs or signals that they were all wrong for each other, and suddenly she loved him so much that she wanted to kill herself if he left her, and blamed herself for not being *classy* enough or horny enough or whatever enough, and couldn't stop crying and drank herself drunk and called him all night long, begging him to reconsider.

Over and Out

He said he felt bad about making her so unhappy but he still packed up and moved three thousand miles away and she didn't die and when he eventually visited her in Los Angeles (she had left Yale and was living with another guy by then, although she wasn't exactly crazy about him either), she couldn't even remember why she had loved Miles Standish MacGregor, and didn't want his tongue or any other part of his anatomy anywhere near her, and wished he would turn around and go right back to Santa Cruz where he was living with another teacher he eventually married.

Conclusion

Romantic love is fleeting. (Okay, it's a cliché, you needn't point that out to me, but it's still true.) The only way to hold onto that kind of love is to kill yourself like Romeo and Juliet when you're still in the throes of passion. If you don't believe me, just imagine Mr. and Mrs. Romeo Montague five years down the pike when he's addicted to internet porn and paunchy from too much Budweiser and she's pregnant with the third kid and has a chronic backache that's making her homicidal. Let's see what Mr. Will-I-Wrote-Hamlet-For-Fuck's-Sake-Shakespeare could do with *that* tragedy.

Not that anyone's advocating suicide. (Please! I don't want to see some creepy Facebook announcement that you took a dive into an empty pool on *my* say-so.) It's just that love is like a three-scoop hot fudge sundae. It's great at the beginning but by the time you get down to the third scoop, the ice cream has turned to soup, the hot fudge is cold, and you feel sick to your stomach from all the nuts and whipped cream.

Of course that's just one opinion. *Your* experience might be entirely different.

Falling Off the Turnip Truck

Listen, I grew up watching movies about Hollywood heartbreak. And you could say my parents were show biz casualties. My ex-husband crashed and burned (symbolically) during the production of his first (and only) feature film. And the big screenplay sale I'd worked 17 years to make marked the end of my screenwriting career. I had even spent a year and a half reading scripts for two rotund producers I named Humpty and Dumpty, who made me page them at The Polo Lounge in order that other, more important producers would hear their names over the loudspeaker. So I wasn't wet behind the ears, and I hadn't just fallen off the turnip truck when I got my second job in Hollywood–Director of Development at Columbia Pictures Television–Syndication.

In case you're wondering what syndication is, this is how my new boss Henry explained it at a dinner party when the woman next to him asked what he did.

"I recycle garbage," he said, smiling devilishly at his girlfriend Libby, who smacked him in the head with her napkin and denied him access (so I'm told) to her body later that night.

"What Henry means," Libby explained grandly, her face a perfect heart-shaped cameo, "is that he sells great series like *The Mary Tyler Moore Show* and *I Love Lucy* to local stations in cities all over America, Europe, Asia and South America so that people can watch and enjoy them for years to come."

"Why, Libby," Henry said, sitting back in his chair to admire her, "I had no idea how important I am."

"Well, you are, so stop being an asshole."

That little lapse in good taste betrayed how recently Libby had risen to prominence as the mistress of a Hollywood mogul.

But I digress.

As a job perk to me for becoming the Director of Development, Henry, a little leprechaun of a man with a reputation for being a dick, announced that he was sending me to Las Vegas to 'get my feet wet.'

"I don't want wet feet," I pleaded. "Please don't send me to Las Vegas. I hate Las Vegas."

"Don't be silly. Everybody loves Las Vegas."

That's how I ended up at the all night fur salon at The

Las Vegas Hilton in the fall of 1979.

The Las Vegas of fashion, glamour, Broadway shows and gourmet dining did not exist in 1979. I was in the Las Vegas of tourists from Tulsa in plaid Bermuda shorts and size XXXL T-shirts who stared in genuine wonder at the giant animatron of the giggling chef in front of Benihana of Tokyo; the tourists who today are more likely to turn up in Branson or DollyWood.

In 1979, these same tourists, together with their cousins, uncles and in-laws from Fargo, Tupelo and Tallahassee, flocked to the 9 o'clock Wayne Newton Show at The Aladdin. And having nothing better to do, I followed the crowd. Before that night, I had no clue about this handsome, charismatic Mr. Las Vegas who, with playful patter, hokey jokes, and a big velvety voice held his audience spellbound for over an hour, three times a night. It captured my imagination, which immediately went to work.

When I got back to the Hilton, I was still jazzed about Wayne Newton and didn't feel like going up to my room. But since I didn't gamble, or drink, and the novelty of being mistaken for a hooker by some sixty-year-old guy in a lime green polyester leisure suit had worn off pretty quickly, I decided to check out the all night fur salon.

Betty, the salon's mistress of the night shift, was a retired Harrah's show girl with straw blond hair, a taut leather face and a tall, trim figure framed in black sequins. Five nights a week, she spent the hours from 11 to 7 filling a large ceramic ashtray with ruby-rimmed Marlboro butts.

I drifted around the salon for a while, burying my fingertips in the lush pile of silver fox, mink, sable and chinchilla. All the really expensive items were locked onto their hangers, but Betty unlocked the ranch mink sweatshirt ($2500) and let me try it on.

"Jesus, Betty, does anyone ever come in and buy something?" I asked, reluctantly returning the sweatshirt after I'd paraded around the store in it.

"Oh, sure," she said in a gravelly voice perfected by decades of tobacco and Jim Beam. "Just last Tuesday, a silver haired gentleman came in with his girlfriend and bought her a beautiful mink jacket. She was just thrilled." Betty laughed a little before transitioning into a long, phlegmmy cough.

We sat quietly for several minutes, zoning out on the Muzak from the corridor and the distant sounds of a band playing "Hang On, Sloopy."

"Say, Betty, do you ever watch The Lawrence Welk Show?"

"Oh, sure," she said, "My mom just loves Lawrence."

"Did you know he's about to retire?" I had read this the week before in *Variety*.

"Is that so?" Her voice sounded concerned but her face didn't move.

"What does your mother think of Wayne Newton?"

"Oh, she just loves him."

"Do you think she'd be happy if Wayne took over for Lawrence?"

"Well, that would be just wonderful. When is Wayne going to do that?"

"Maybe soon."

"Well, that would be wonderful."

Good old Betty, my one-woman focus group. I had made my first sale!

The good news was that Henry loved the idea. More importantly, Libby, for whom Henry had left his wife of 25 years, loved it, too. Nothing happened in our division without Libby's blessing.

"I'm going to give myself a raise," he said.

"Why should *you* get a raise?" I demanded.

"I hired you. I sent you to Vegas. And I'm the boss."

The bad news was that Henry sent me back to Las Vegas to float the idea past Wayne Newton. But he didn't think my feet were wet enough yet for a big celebrity, so he sent along Ed McDonald, the VP of Development, as heavy artillery. I liked Ed well enough, and he was a good mentor, but a few weeks earlier at an industry cocktail party, after his fourth Glenfiddich and soda, he had tearfully confessed that his wife's slipped disk precluded sexual intercourse and begged me to sleep with him.

Hoping to avoid an encore, I was relieved when Ed flew in by himself. I had not been on a plane since my daughter was born in 1967, so I took the overnight Greyhound Bus which arrived downtown on the old Vegas strip at 4 a.m.

The plan was for me to meet Ed at Newton's place at one in the afternoon because Wayne didn't get up until noon. Which meant I had a whole morning to kill in Bugsy Siegel's bordello of broken dreams.

Determined to dodge Ed, who was hanging out at the Aladdin which Newton owned at the time, I had breakfast next to the bus terminal with a nightshift of exhausted waitresses, dime-bag drug peddlers and bruised and bloated hookers at a raunchy café that smelled like burnt bacon. Fortunately, I had brought along a fabulous old novel about naked ambition in Hollywood, Bud Schulburg's *What Makes Sammy Run*, which, together with my nerves, helped keep me awake until meeting time.

The cab ride to Wayne Newton's home provided a tour of greater Las Vegas. Once we left the casinos behind, the city looked like Barstow and every other flat, dusty desert town on the I-15. There were clusters of ranch style tract houses, an occasional shopping mall, some churches and banks, the usual fast food franchises, the scattered buildings of a high school with a large athletic field and then nothing but cactus and sand–allegedly the mob's favorite burial ground.

After a fifteen minute drive, the cab driver entered Newton's gated estate. Once inside, the landscape transformed from Kansas to Oz. There were luxurious stretches of well-watered grass, manicured bushes, established trees, proliferations of flowers and a series of increasingly impressive houses, each separated by a substantial portion of land. Along the way, we passed an enormous, brightly painted barn and a sprawling pasture where at least 20 horses and their offspring grazed.

"Arabians," the cab driver commented. He had been inside the estate before.

"Who lives in all these houses?"

"The ones who work for Mr. Newton," the driver, an old Mexican with high Indian cheekbones, answered, sounding proud, as if he were a member of Newton's family.

"Where is Mr. Newton's house?"

"You'll see. It is very great."

It was far and away the finest of all the other houses, a colonial two stories high with a sweeping circular driveway, and an enormous fountain in which three stone nymphs frolicked lasciviously.

As I entered the front door, I was overtaken by a maid, a butler and two friendly Great Danes the size of Shetland ponies. The interior seemed determined to disguise its newness and emulate the great old money mansions of Grosse Pointe, Atlanta, or San Marino. Everywhere I looked there was highly polished wood, antique crystal chandeliers, oriental rugs, elegant print upholstery, heavy drapes half-drawn to admit light without heat, and immense furniture–

as if giants lived there.

I was led by the butler into a study, where Ed, wearing a new charcoal gray suit which minimized his stout body, was waiting.

"Not bad, huh?" he said softly as I took a seat beside him.

"It's good to be the king."

Newton, smiling warmly, swept into the room half an hour late, accompanied by the maid who carried a silver coffee service to a round table in the center of the room. He greeted us using our first names, settled unceremoniously onto the enormous sofa opposite us, rather than sitting behind his palatial desk, and made certain that we had already been offered refreshments before the maid poured his coffee.

Wearing a loose, sky blue crewneck sweater, black flannel trousers, and loafers without socks, he seemed very congenial, listening quietly and without impatience to my ten-minute pitch.

After I had finished, he asked a few intelligent questions–who would produce and direct (he had a few suggestions, which Ed wrote down), hour-long or hour-and-a-half (hour-long), how many shows would he be committing to per season (12, but there could be 8 if 12 conflicted with his Aladdin commitments), a live audience (naturally), dancers (probably), big name guests stars (absolutely).

"You know, my audience is younger than Lawrence Welk's," Newton said.

"Of course," Ed said. "That's exactly the point, Wayne. Welk's audience is elderly. We need a successor who'll attract a younger audience. That's you. There's no other contender."

"Okay," Newton said brightly, standing up and coming over to us. Ed sprang up quickly to shake his hand, grasping Newton's elbow with his other hand.

"We want your input every step of the way," Ed said. "This is your baby, and we want you to have whatever you want."

"Great. Bernie wanted to be here today but he had a big meeting in New York. Talk to him. Tell him I'm on board. If he likes the deal, let's move forward."

With that, Newton escorted us out into the hallway, shaking hands with both of us. The butler led us back to the two-story entryway, past 19th century European landscapes in ornate gold frames. Outside the front door, a limousine was waiting to take us back to town.

An early evening bus carried me home to L.A. Practically dancing inside my skin, I was impervious to body odors, bathroom smells, baby screams and sonic snores. The news flash was that I had come up with a *high concept* all by myself and sold it! My escape from anonymity, I calculated, was only months away. Of course, a syndicated Saturday night series was not the kind of success I had anticipated, but it was a doorway to bankability. I began to free associate about the house I wanted, definitely a big view beauty in the Hollywood Hills with wide plank rosewood floors, a master suite with a room-sized closet for me, a play suite for my daughter, and a gourmet kitchen equipped with stainless steel appliances and crowned by skylights. And maybe I'd buy an Arabian–hell, Wayne might even give me one in gratitude after we won a Best Variety Show Emmy. Exhausted, I fell into a featherbed of sweet dreams.

What happened next was that Business Affairs was supposed to draw up a deal memo for Wayne to sign, followed somewhere down the line by a formal contract. In the meantime, Ed and I went ahead with the production plans, preparing a budget, hiring the producer, director, and writers. They would create the pilot script, hire their staff, and book the guest stars, while the set designer, costume designer and lighting designer developed the look of the show. These people in turn would hire the hundred or so other people needed for an hour-long production, actors for the sketches, a choreographer and dancers for the production numbers, cameramen, drivers, grips, gaffers, assistants, and the caterer. And so on. Columbia invested close to a million dollars in the pre-pro during the next seven weeks.

Five days before the pilot was scheduled to be shot, Wayne Newton's people informed us that he had decided to accept a network deal for four ABC specials instead of doing Columbia's syndicated series.

I was outraged. How could Newton back out of a deal he had agreed to? What about the Business Affairs deal memo he had signed?

There had been no deal memo; Business Affairs, backed up with other show deals, had dropped the ball. In the next weeks, we learned that the meeting which Bernie, Newton's agent, had attended in New York was with ABC. Good old Bernie had most likely used the Columbia series as a negotiating ploy to get the Specials. And since Newton believed, according to Bernie, that network specials were more prestigious than a syndicated series, naturally he chose ABC.

Nobody at Columbia was particularly upset. What I perceived as a devastating betrayal was met with a shrug, not a shriek. Business Affairs and Henry received slaps on the wrist for letting it happen, but no one was beheaded or defrocked. The accountants just scratched their heads and wrote it off as a routine business loss.

For me, it felt like a rerun of the time an agent who I thought was my friend told a roomful of executives, including Humpty and Dumpty, that he had never agreed to let Tom Selleck play Clark Gable in a CBS Wednesday night movie, even though he had practically sung love songs to me about the project for over a month. The agent refused to make eye contact with me after I accused him of treachery and when I couldn't get him to recant his lie, I burst into tears in front of everyone. True killers like Bernie and Henry, of course, would have handled this *contretemps* eyeball to eyeball without even flinching.

As fate would have it, none of the Wayne Newton Specials ever aired, on ABC or elsewhere. For all I knew, they weren't even made. And after Lawrence Welk retired, there was no successor. The Saturday early evening variety franchise went by the wayside.

Wayne Newton continued for decades to have sold-out shows in Las Vegas. But he never achieved a presence on television. Henry was eventually edged out of Columbia; he moved with Libby to a mansion in Atlanta, where he worked for Ted Turner. Ed McDonald was forcibly retired; he became an adjunct professor in the Communications Department at CSUN. And I voluntarily left show business, swimming against the current toward the shark free shores of advertising.

Despite my hard boiled pretensions, I fell off the turnip truck and crashed into the Hollywood sign in less than four years. But when all is said and done, I walked away from show business relatively unscathed. I finally sold a screenplay, even though it got shelved. I had my Big Fish That Got Away story about Wayne Newton. And I learned the hard way that a Hollywood handshake is synonymous with the Mafia kiss.

I haven't returned to Hollywood or Las Vegas since 1981, despite a few pricey job offers from the one and an occasional phone solicitation offering me a luxurious, free two-night stay from the other. But I quite enjoy reading stories about both of them. And every once in a while, I sit down and write one.

ʃʃ

Some of this story is true, but most of it is fiction. For one thing, Wayne Newton did not have Great Danes or 19th century European landscapes in his entryway. And the name of his agent wasn't Bernie, although it might have been. And none of these characters ever said any of the dialogue I wrote for them. But there *was* an all night fur salon at The Las Vegas Hilton. And I was actually propositioned by a man in a lime green leisure suit.

Locked in the Bathroom at The Actors Studio

It was October, 1967. I remember because it was exactly three months after I gave birth to my first and only daughter, Desdemona, and I was observing an acting class at The Actors Studio, one of the privileges of being in the Directors' Unit. We were encouraged to watch The Great Man, Lee Strasberg, work with actors as part of our training and, being star struck, I hoped to see Strasberg put someone famous, like Paul Newman, through his paces. Most of the celebrities, however, had long before left for Hollywood by the late sixties, although one, thank God, was back in New York doing a play which she was rehearsing at TAS on that particular day.

Strasberg sat slumped in his directors' chair with a shawl draped over his shoulders like an elderly Jewish woman, alternately coddling and savaging the actors, displaying a shocking degree of favoritism and displeasure, at least in my estimation. One student in particular, a tall, attractive brunette in her late twenties whom he would eventually marry after his wife Paula died, received everything but a bouquet of orchids for her overwrought performance as Madge in a scene from William Inge's *Picnic*, while a young man I thought might be the next Marlon Brando had to settle for grudging praise after his heartrending performance as Biff in an excerpt from Arthur Miller's *Death of a Salesman.* But Strasberg was just warming up. Suddenly he leaped to his feet, flowed onto the stage area, and performed an impromptu diatribe. To my shock and horror, I–who he did not know from Adam–was his target.

"You should fire your hairdresser," he said, referring to my overgrown, copper-colored curls. "It's a good thing for you that the practice of shaving women's heads has been discontinued or you'd be giving Yul Brynner competition, girlie."

He went on for several more minutes about my "clown clothes," savoring his wit and brutality as if he were John Simon, the infamous *New York Magazine* critic who enjoyed skewering actresses like Barbra Streisand and Liza Minelli for their looks.

And when I tried to fight back, saying "Who are you to–," he cut me off, shouting, "*You* don't talk!"

After the class broke, I retreated to the back bathroom of the Studio in tears, feeling like a circus freak. I fastened the little hook on the door securely so nobody could burst in on my misery and dropped down on the toilet with a heavy sigh. There I was, sitting where Brando, Newman, James Dean, Kim Stanley, Genevieve Page, and Marilyn Monroe had bared their bottoms, that levelling process to which all human beings are subjected.

When I finally collected myself, I stood up and looked in the mirror, which was as scratched and battered as the rest of this heralded 44th Street Studio. *What the hell was wrong with the way I looked,* I asked myself. Okay, I wasn't a glamour girl, but I wasn't exactly a troll, either. And since when was becoming a director a beauty contest?

"Desdemona loves me," I said to the mirror, as if Strasberg were hiding behind it, gloating. Suddenly all I wanted to do was to be back home with my daughter and her father, a young filmmaker named Simon Weiss. To hell with directing!

I reached for the door latch and tried to lift up the hook. It wouldn't budge. I stuck my thumb underneath the hook and pushed, but it wouldn't give way. I looked around for something I could use to coax the hook out of the metal loop it was nested in, but there was nothing available. I dumped the contents of my purse onto the cracked and discolored white tiles, searching for anything I could use to force the hook up. My house key looked promising but nothing I did persuaded the hook to move even slightly. I took off one of my shoes and started hammering it, more in frustration than utility, but the hook remained jammed inside its little circular cradle, perhaps for eternity. In desperation, I used my thumb again and this time the hook pierced the skin, digging deep into my flesh. A fat blood droplet appeared, followed by a rosy parade. I grabbed a wad of toilet paper and made a makeshift bandage, but it quickly soaked through. If I didn't bleed to death, I'd probably end up with tetanus.

I considered the little window. If worse came to worst, I could climb out, jumping down into the alley behind the studio, although probably breaking a foot in the process. But when I tried to open it, the frame was hopelessly imbedded in decades of thick white paint.

Panic set in. I began to shout, "Help! Please someone help me!" I heard voices in the hallway, but nobody replied. I shouted again. "I'm locked in the bathroom. Please, someone, help me!"

There was some high pitched laughter.

What the hell was going on? Was there a Studio-wide vendetta against me?

I sat back down on the toilet. What would Desdemona's father tell her, I wondered, when she was old enough to understand why I hadn't come home? "Your mother got locked in a famous show business bathroom and she died, Desy. There was a nice little item about it with her picture in *The New York Times*."

I became a Crisis Christian that afternoon, one of those hypocrites who only pray to God when they're in trouble. Oh, Lord, why did I have to be so ambitious, I asked. Why wasn't I satisfied to be a mother and a playwright and an award-winning advertising copywriter?

When God didn't answer, I resumed shouting, cursing and pleading. Then it dawned on me: people must think I was rehearsing! Countless times I'd heard actors off in some corner or coat closet or anywhere else they could secure a little privacy, crying, moaning, shrieking, swearing, *preparing*–and I'd paid no attention.

"*I'm not rehearsing*!" I shouted. "This is not a rehearsal!"

The indistinct chatter in the hallway stopped.

"I'm locked in the bathroom!" I cried out.

A woman's voice said, "Okay."

"Not okay."

"I'll get help."

A few moments later, something flat and metallic slid under the door.

"Use it like a crowbar," a man's voice said. Men were always saying ridiculous things like "use it like a crowbar," as if a woman would know what a crowbar was, let alone what to do with it.

"How?" I howled.

"Wedge it under the curve of the hook and pump. Like a car jack."

Another entirely unhelpful simile.

I shoved. Nothing. I shoved and lifted. *Nada.* The third time, I emitted a little cry of despair as I shoved and lifted. That must have done the trick.

The hook popped up and the door swung open, revealing three actors in the hallway, one of whom was Madeleine Sherwood, the mother of the no-neck monsters in *Cat on A Hot Tin Roof.*

"Are you okay?" she asked, peering at me through thick bifocals that were attached to a braided ribbon around her neck.

I started to cry.

"It happens all the time," the tall young actor next to her said. His was the voice that had guided me. "They ought to fix it," he said, easing the makeshift crowbar from my bloody hand, which had been grasping it like the Holy Grail.

Madeleine Sherwood reached into an enormous straw carry-all and handed me a tissue.

"Come with me," she said, leading me toward the Studio's little kitchen. "You look like you need a drink."

I hoped she was referring to alcohol, but what she had in mind was water, ice cold, from a jug in the refrigerator. I drank it greedily, not realizing until that moment how thirsty I'd become during my captivity.

I never returned to The Actor's Studio after that traumatic afternoon, although twenty years later I would spend a year in the Playwriting Unit at The Actors Studio West. I recall one of those evenings in LA when I desperately needed to pee, having eaten a particularly salty bowl of *matzoh* ball soup at Jerry's Famous Deli, followed by two chardonnays and several glasses of water. But like a skittish horse who avoids a particular trail where he once tripped and fell, I crossed my legs tightly while playwright Paul Zindel lectured on the necessity of employing dramaturgy when you write drama, and with fierce determination I held my *own* horses in check for the next two hours.

MAUSCHWITZ

The day you discover you are capable of hatred can be quite exhilarating. It means you no longer have to pretend to emulate Mother Teresa or Melanie Wilkes. You can be racist when the Korean woman in front of you is driving 11 mph in the fast lane. You can be rude when two Seventh Day Adventists in unfashionable blue suits want to introduce you to Jesus. You can refuse to return phone calls to people who bore you, even if they're suicidal. And you can walk past paraplegics, amputees and alcoholics without fumbling in your purse for a quarter.

The day I accepted how much I hated Ed Frankel, the monastery doors burst open. And when I learned a year later that he had died and I was glad, I burned my hair shirt. I was no longer going to feel ashamed of the devil who partied inside of me. After all, even Martin Luther admitted that Satan lived in his ass.

Ed Frankel, a short, muscular fellow with good hair and a tense jaw, got on my bad side when I was creative director of an ad agency that handled Disney's home video library, and he was "the client." I had encountered my share of asshole clients, as everyone does who works in advertising. There was the ice cream client who said our ads were too creative for a small space. There was the owner of a chain of health clubs who thought the black and white monitor he was watching meant that we weren't shooting his commercials in color. Then there was the deli owner who mistook the rough drawings of his mile-high sandwiches in the layouts for finished ads, yelling that we had made the meat look like shit. Not to mention the golf club client who fell asleep watching his expensive new 30-second commercial, "The Ball that Flew to the Moon." But Ed Frankel wasn't unsophisticated, cowardly or sleepy. He was a sadist.

"Let's see your latest waste of time and money," he'd say at the beginning of a meeting just as a warm-up insult. Our account executive Buddy Darrow would chuckle obsequiously, mopping his bulbous red alcoholic's nose with a hanky as he accidentally spilled the storyboards onto the floor.

"What a kidder, Ed," I'd say, retrieving the storyboards and wishing that the scenery truck rumbling past the building was a prelude to The Big One.

On the day before Thanksgiving, Ed crowed, "Congratulations, Dani. You've managed to do the impossible. You've wrecked *Bambi*!"

The nicest thing Ed ever said about us was, "Well, you hire shit, you get shit. Go ahead and finish it."

It got so bad that once, after he kept us waiting in the hall for over two hours, I walked out, leaving poor, gin-starved Buddy and the creative team standing there with their mouths hanging open.

Of course, the general manager of our agency, Todd Berger, called me on the carpet the next day. He was rocking back and forth on his wingtips, his usually-tanned face as red as Buddy's nose.

"You had no right to walk out, Dani. I don't give a crap how long that putz kept you waiting."

"He's a miserable little faggot, Todd. He hates the world and he takes it out on us."

"I don't care if he's the fuckin' queen of Romania, you have to stand there and take it. He's our second biggest client. He pays your salary!"

"Yes, I know. So we're just a bunch of whores, right?"

"Is that news?"

Before Ed Frankel, I thought of Disney as a great opportunity. I had desperately wanted to be a Mousketeer like Annette Funicello when I was 8. And like most other kids in the 50's, I had grown up loving *Snow White*, *Pinnochio*, *Dumbo*, *Cinderella*, and *Bambi*. What a privilege, I thought, to edit the footage of these masterpieces into irresistible four-color, 30-second enticements. Bring Bambi Home! Let Dumbo Take You Flying! I was such a fan that it startled me when a disgruntled screenwriter dubbed Disney Studios "Mauschwitz." But Ed Frankel was my exit visa from Fantasyland.

I was not a happy camper when Todd Berger informed me that we, the agency *we*, were going to attend Ed Frankel's funeral, and that I, agency creative director, was going to write–and deliver–a tribute to the rotten sonovabitch.

"We are not going to lose this account just because Frankel is dead and some new asshole wants an agency that *he* has chosen! We are going to wow them with a great tribute that features our devotion to Disney Home Video, our beloved client. And you are going to make a winning wowee."

"A winning wowee?" I repeated, holding the phrase in my mouth like a spoiled oyster. "Gee, Todd, you're making me want to puke."

"Get over it."

I sat in front of my computer, staring at the working title of the tribute: "Ding Dong. The Bitch is Dead." Where was Hannah Arendt when I needed her? Reaching into the trash for my compassion, I tried to think of Ed's grieving parents, but all I could conjure up were two drag queens, one sobbing sloppily, the other poking her in the ribs and shrieking, "Stop, Henrietta, stop!"

The Evil Queen from *Snow White* hallucinated her way

into my office, wanting to be paid off for delivering Ed the poison apple. She leaned so close, I could smell her stringy hair and that awful sour perfume called "Old Flesh." I asked if she'd take a check.

Jake, the art director on the account, wandered into my office wearing a merciless little grin, his hair sticking straight up in the air like an Iroquois brave. "How's it going?"

"How do you think?"

"Yeah," Jake acknowledged, still grinning. He had purple jelly on the side of his mouth from the doughnut he was munching "Did you know Ed died of AIDS?"

"Awww, shit, don't tell me that."

"Maybe it'll help you write the tribute," Jake said, pulling another doughnut out of a white deli bag.

"Thanks a bunch. Why couldn't he have been hit by a tour bus crossing the lot to his car?"

"Nope, it was AIDS. Another one bites the dust, as Freddie Mercury would say."

"Go away, Jake."

Another one bites the dust. I liked that. Scrolling backwards to the working title, I changed it.

The ghost of Ollie floated in from the bright windows behind my desk, irresistibly seductive Ollie, dead at 40 of AIDS. "Hi, kids," he said, dropping his lanky, prepped-out body into a convenient chair. "I'm bored. Make me laugh."

"Have you come to torment me?"

"How's your love life?"

"He dumped me."

"Awwwwww."

"I see that death has not improved your narcissism."

"What did you think of my memorial service?" he asked, wetting his finger with his tongue and rubbing a white spot off his Gucci loafers.

"It was a 50 share."

Crazy Cheryl, Ollie's favorite heterosexual playmate when he was screwing up his relationship with Peter, presided over the service, sporting a wacky purple hat with ostrich feathers and faux lynx fur that Ollie had picked out for her.

"Controlling everything as usual," she said, grabbing hold of the hat for emphasis. We all laughed, recalling with mixed emotions what a control freak he was. That was, in fact, what drove us apart. Ollie had insisted upon calling my married boyfriend Jeff to tell him to leave his wife for me and no amount of begging would stop him. I just couldn't handle his lunacy any longer, especially when I was being encouraged by a brace of therapists to grab hold of my sanity. I didn't know that he had been diagnosed with AIDS and was probably acting manic to avoid his terror of dying. I didn't realize when he knocked his water glass out of my hand at our favorite restaurant on Larchmont that he was trying to protect me from contagion. So I dropped him, and two years later he died without me. Fortunately, he had several hundred other friends, most of whom had stuck around, and they all piled into the big white church on Franklin Avenue for his memorial. When I looked around, the only significant person I didn't see was Peter.

I couldn't cry, even when I stood up to tell what had happened to us and how much I envied everyone else in the room for having thicker skins. But when Claire, Ollie's beloved you-should-excuse-the-expression fag hag, lumbered over to hug me after the ceremony, with her hideously permed blond frizz and her 250 pound body tightly packed into a yellow floral pup tent, I burst into tears, as if the pain of losing my closest friend had been warehoused somewhere out in Arcadia and required some time in a truck to be retrieved. Or maybe I just needed somebody kind to hug me.

I looked back at the computer screen. It still said "Another one bites the dust." I pushed delete. Then I typed in "Sympathy for the Devil." Now I was really depressed, and it was all Ed Frankel's fault. Fuck him, I thought, and then felt guilty. Fuck that little weasel for dying of AIDS and making me feel bad for hating him.

I wasn't sure how to dress for the Frankel memorial service. I decided on a navy blue suit with a white blouse, low heels, and pearls. In the bedroom mirror, I looked like the second-most-likely-to-succeed Republican candidate's wife. Actually, I looked like my ex-boyfriend Jeff's wife, except for the face. She was a proud Daughter of the American Revolution, a Martha Washington look-alike for whom pearls were a permanent scarification.

I couldn't eat, I was too nervous, but I thought I should shove something down my throat so that I didn't have a hypoglycemic attack and pass out while I was speaking. I settled for an apple, which turned out to be grainy and tasted like semi-sweet sand. I washed it down with a Diet Coke and emitted a loud belch.

"That was ladylike," I commented to the dog, feeling like an imposter in my church clothes.

Parking was impossible, as it always is in West Hollywood. I couldn't even find a pay parking lot, just on-street metered parking, of which there was none available, and side street parking, which was illegal without a permit. I ended up leaving the car in a Pavilions lot six blocks from the church, going into the store and coming out another door in case a parking guard was watching.

I was late by the time I reached the church. The minister was already speaking about Ed and his beloved parents, Elsie and Donald Frankel. I strained to catch sight of them; neither was in drag.

I crept down a side aisle, looking for the familiar agency faces. They were 12 rows back, right off the aisle, and hadn't saved me a seat, the bastards. I found a single vacant one in the 11th row and struggled to maneuver past the mourners without stepping on someone's foot.

Sighing with relief as I settled into the seat, I turned to

look at Todd. He shook his head and squeezed his mouth into a disapproving smirk. Jake was grinning at me like a caged monkey, his diarrhea-brown sport jacket straining to hold his belly in place.

There didn't seem to be any formal order for the speakers. Each one walked down front, stepped onto a raised dais, spoke, and returned to his seat, followed by a pause until the next person got up. If I waited long enough, I thought desperately, perhaps the minister would end the service before I could speak. But Todd had no intention of letting that happen. He tapped me sharply on the shoulder and whispered, "Get your ass down there." I started to rise, but then someone else appeared at the front of the church. He looked to be in his early thirties with a thin face made thinner by a blond brush cut. Was this Ed's lover? He was wearing a black suit, white shirt and a red plaid bow-tie, which made him look like grandma's favorite little boy, or an undertaker. It was hard to hear him because he spoke softly, but I caught some of it. Ed was an amazing friend who was always there to listen whenever he needed him. *Ed*? Was he kidding? Then he said that Ed had been very brave about the diagnosis, maintaining his sense of humor even when his t-cell count dipped below 100. Ed had a sense of humor? He said that he loved Ed and would probably never find a better friend. He started to cry a little. Feeling embarrassed, I looked down at my lap, discovering that I had unwittingly shredded part of the little speech I had prepared. But I could still make out most of the words;

it was just the paper that looked damp and worm-eaten.

When Ed's friend finished speaking, Todd poked me in the neck with his finger. I shot up, stumbled over to the aisle, and started to walk forward. My legs were shaking. Oh my God, this was going to be a disaster.

At the dais, I tried to smooth out the paper. My hands were shaking as badly as my legs. People started to cough uncomfortably. Adjusting the microphone, I forced myself to speak.

"My name is Dani Lauer. I am the creative director at Sweeney and Markowitz, the agency which handles the Disney Home Video account. Ed Frankel was my client." My voice sounded shrill and wobbly, like Eleanor Roosevelt's. I took a deep breath.

"We were thrilled to have the privilege of working on such masterpieces as *Snow White*, *Pinnochio* and *Cinderella.* Ed was a very demanding boss, asking for our very finest work and never settling for less. The payoff was that Disney Home Video scored a hit every time an animation classic was released." Todd had made me put that in, to remind the Disney execs what a great job we'd done for them.

The next line was, "We will miss Ed." I started to say it, but I couldn't finish. Everything became blurry and I felt light-headed. Then something gushed out of me like an episode of "I Didn't Know I was Pregnant."

"Listening to Ed's friends speak about him today, I realize that I . . . didn't really know him. To be honest," I said, wondering what I was going to be honest about, "the Ed I knew was–well, he could be very . . . harsh." My legs had stopped shaking, but I couldn't bring myself to look up from the paper I was no longer reading. "I think that Ed–well, he never minced words with me. So–today I haven't, either. Maybe he would have liked that." There was really nothing left to say. "Thank you very much for letting me speak. I am really, uh, . . . very sorry for your loss."

The oxygen began returning to my brain. Oh my god, I thought, I'm going to be fired. Avoiding everyone's gaze, I hurried back to my seat, stumbling on the carpet and nearly falling before a man grabbed my arm to steady me. I glanced at him for a second, gratefully. He nodded and gave me a little smile.

When I sat down again, I began to cry. I couldn't stop the tears, but I struggled not to make a sound. I felt a hand gently squeeze my shoulder. I patted the hand without turning around.

I didn't lose my job. And we didn't lose the account. A woman named Harriet took over for Ed and everything went on as if nothing had happened. Advertising was like that. People came and went, dropping off the edge of the world like it was really flat after all, and it didn't seem to matter if they were important or not, everyone went over the edge eventually, blip-blip-blip. I didn't particularly like Harriet, she wasn't smart like Ed and didn't push us very hard. But she was never mean, just dim. Her highest praise was, "That's cute." Jake began using that expression whenever we presented something internally. "Oh, that's so cute," he would shriek, "isn't that the cutest thing?"

I don't usually think about Ed unless I bump into one of the old Disney classics on TV. Then I remember something cutting he said to me, like "Well, Snow White you're not," but it doesn't bother me like it used to. Mauschwitz is gone, at least for me, deserted and windblown like any disaster area reinvented by time; all the bodies are buried in the ash pond and a ragged grass has taken over. I have made my peace with Disney as the not-so-magical kingdom. I have even resumed a half-hearted quest to emulate Melanie Wilkes, or Mother Teresa–but only after she admitted that she had lost her faith. To be honest, I miss how exhilarating it felt to be a real sonovabitch for a while. Ed gave me that. He was like a colon cleanse that swept out all the bullshit-caked pipes, the politically correct orifices, and scrubbed them honest. Maybe that's what bad guys do for us. Maybe that's why we hold onto them–Satan for the Christians, Haman for the Jews, the Mafia for all of us who crave a little anarchy. It's like Oppenheimer said after the first atom bomb test, "Now we're all sons of bitches."

Let's face it, the dark side is a far more popular vacation resort than Disney World. It might not be a bad idea to purchase a timeshare there.

Brandon French is the only daughter of an opera singer and a Spanish dancer, born in Chicago sometime after The Great Fire of 1871. She has been (variously) assistant editor of *Modern Teen Magazine*, a topless Pink Pussycat cocktail waitress, an assistant professor of English at Yale, a published film scholar, playwright and screenwriter, Director of Development at Columbia Pictures Television, an award-winning advertising copywriter and Creative Director, a psychoanalyst in private practice, and a mother. Sixty-three of her stories have been accepted for publication by literary journals and anthologies, she's been nominated twice for a Pushcart, she was an award winner in the 2015 *Chicago Tribune* Nelson Algren Short Story Contest, and she has a previously published collection of poetry entitled *Pie*.

CPSIA information can be obtained
at www.ICGtesting.com
Printed in the USA
FSHW011548240819
61391FS